LETTERS TO GRAND CHILDREN

by Elaine Mayer

Order this book online at www.trafford.com
or email orders@trafford.com

Most Trafford titles are also available at major online book retailers.

Printed in Victoria, BC, Canada.

ISBN: 978-1-4269-1542-0 (sc)
ISBN: 978-1-4269-1541-3 (dj)

Library of Congress Control Number: 2009934603

Our mission is to efficiently provide the world's finest, most comprehensive book publishing service, enabling every author to experience success. To find out how to publish your book, your way, and have it available worldwide, visit us online at www.trafford.com

Trafford rev. 3/31/2010

Trafford PUBLISHING®   www.trafford.com

North America & international
toll-free: 1 888 232 4444 (USA & Canada)
phone: 250 383 6864 ♦ fax: 812 355 4082

These letters are for Grand Children everywhere, all ages and conditions.

AUTHOR'S NOTE

Our Grand Children live in San Diego, Denver, Twin Cities, Milwaukee, and Winnipeg, a nice route for someone who has the leisure to travel but for me it is not nearly enough, so to keep in touch I wrote these *Letters to Grand Children* and sent them via email.

These letters look at how our lives are shaped by people and nature, how the world and everything in it is part of our ancestry. It is an attempt to awaken them to the natural world and her doorways that connect us to the Spiritual realm. It offers another way of interpreting the world's signs and wonders.

My intention is for them to understand that they are a part of holy creation, integral with Earth whose gifts of air, water, soil, and all forms of life are the web in which we live.

Thomas Berry, CP, writes, "We seem unable to deal with the universe itself as the primary revelation of the divine before there ever was any Bible and as the context in which the Bible itself needs to be interpreted. We are concerned with the Genesis story that we know through reading, not with the story of the universe that we know through observation."

Our ancient ancestors observed their world and understood that they were holy in a sacred home. They depended on Mother Earth and Father Sun. They were acquainted with the mysteries of birth and death. Being familiar with the seasons of the year, they experienced renewal/ resurrection/ transformation. Eucharist was celebrated at every meal. They respected their plant and animal cousins and thanked those spirits that gave their lives for humankind. To them, air was the breath of the divine. Observing the mystical Universe gave them the foundation for their imagination and creativity.

Threads of these truths are found in all major faith traditions and philosophies. Since the intimate-interdependent-developing universe is our first and most basic revelation about the web of life woven by the Cosmic Dreamer, faith traditions are subordinate to it.

The miracles in nature surpass religious doctrines even as those doctrines nurture and continue to influence us in our search for the Divine. This truth beyond "creeds" generates convergence and unity and infinite possibilities. We can recognize our interdependence and need for each other on the path of healing, or we can languish in fear and distrust on the path of destruction. This message has infiltrated the world's cultures through all ages, but the path of healing is gaining strength today. I want our grandchildren to know that this is happening.

Many of these letters return to the First Scripture, to Nature, where our senses search out Holy Wisdom. We all are Grand Children who are touched by the Source of Love when we see Earth's goodness, smell the pungency of creation, feel the breath of the Spirit, taste life in its diversity, and hear the music of the universe.

Elaine Mayer

ACKNOWLEDGEMENTS

Without the suggestion, encouragement and advice of my husband, Joe, this book never would have happened. We began our journey together on June 13, 1959, bringing our generations of ancestry with us. Since then, we have been joined by our children and grandchildren, and many friends who have been critical to us and the formation of the book. Some of those friends we have met through our reading; Thomas Berry, Brian Swimme, Cletus Wessels, Karen Armstrong, Riane Eisler, John Shelby Spong, Elaine Pagels, John Dominic Crossan, Val Webb, Elizabeth Schusler Fiorenza, and the list can go on.

Our newest friends, the staff at Trafford Publishing, have given the book a face. It truly belongs to all of us, or more appropriately, to the Universe.

Mayer Family - Front: Teresa (Kress), J. Urban, Marie, Tony
Back: Dick, Lawrence "Lorne," Joe, Jack, Mary (Jenney)

June 13, 1959

Mraz Family - Front: Elaine (Mayer), Carolyn (Kucera), Mary (Martin)
Back: Mark, Chuck, Steve, Mike

FAMILY TREE

Joseph Urban **MAYER** (Sept 5, 1903–Oct 24, 1990) and Marie **KLEIN** (Mar 12, 1908–July 1, 1999) married May 22, 1934
Joseph "Joe" *May 14, 1935) married Elaine
John "Jack" (June 27, 1936-Oct 27, 2003) married Barbara
Lawrence "Lorne" (Oct 8, 1937) married Jan
Richard "Dick" (Feb 15, 1940) married Jane
Mary (Nov 30, 1941) Married Bill
Teresa (Aug 5, 1943–May 23, 2006) married Mike
Anthony "Tony" (July 16, 1946) married Linda

Charles **MRAZ** (July 2, 1910–July 12, 1985) and Mildred **ERNST** (April 29, 1912–June 23, 1957) married July 9, 1934)
Elaine (June 8, 1935) married Joe
Carolyn (Nov 7, 1938) married Tony
Charles Ernst "Chuck" (Sept 27, 1940–Sept 15, 1994) married Leanna
Mary (Dec 14, 1945) married Richard
Stephan "Steve" (Sept 24, 1948) married Barbara
Mark (Oct 6, 1950) married Faye
Michael "Mike" (Nov 3, 1953) married Dede and later divorced; married Edie

Joseph "Joe" **MAYER** (May 14, 1935) and Elaine **MRAZ** (June 8, 1935) married June 13, 1959
Teresa (Feb 7, 1961) married Glen Redpath Oct 1987 (divorced)
• Connor (Aug 1, 1993)
• Eamon (Mar 22, 1996)
Married Chris Youngdahl Mar 21, 2006
        • Shea (Feb 20, 1988)
        • Kaylee (Mar 9, 1989)

Joseph Charles "Joe" (Feb 23, 1962) married Marlena Jackman Aug 1986 (separated 2004)
- Kelli (Sept 22, 1991)
- Joseph Donald "JD" (July 15, 1993)
Married Molly Keogh Sept 2007
    - Buddy (June 14, 1992)
    - Caitie (Oct 19, 1994)

Rebecca "Becky" (Sept 15, 1963) married Michael Maniaci June 2001
    - Ren (July 31, 1986)
- Jackson (May 24, 2005)

Andrew "Andy" (Sept 30, 1965) married Ann Donohue June, 1990
- Patricia (Dec 4, 1992)
- Caroline (Dec 27, 1993)
- Tim (April 19, 1996)

Mary Beth "Mary" (Mar 12, 1968) married John Weidner June 1993
- John Christopher (April 17, 1997)
- Elizabeth "Ellie" (May 30, 1999)

Jennifer "Jen" (May 26, 1971) married Lee Greseth Aug 1995
- Morgan (May 13, 2003)
- Luke (June 29, 2005)

Sarah (Feb 5, 1975) married Michael Bird Nov 2006
- Sophia Elaine (April 23, 2009)

Benjamin "Ben" (Mar 4, 1978) friend Erica Powell

TABLE OF CONTENTS

1.	Genesis	1
2.	At the Cottage	3
3.	Thanksgiving	5
4.	Advent	7
5.	Magic	9
6.	Martin Luther King Day	11
7.	Sarah's Birthday	13
8.	Honeybees	15
9.	Teresa's Birthday	17
10.	Lent and Spring	20
11.	St. Valentines	22
12.	Eagle Watching	24
13.	Enchanting Sunday	26
14.	Violence in School	28
15.	Uncle Joe's Birthday	30
16.	Precious Earth	32
17.	Earthlings	34
18.	Rediscover our Unity	36
19.	Ben's Birthday	38
20.	Mary's Birthday	40
21.	San Diego	43
22.	Leprechauns and St Patrick	45
23.	Wedding	47
24.	Easter Thoughts	49
25.	Tsunami	51
26.	Wakanhezas	53
27.	Snow and Creative Juices	55
28.	Family Excursions	57
29.	Mother's Day	58
30.	Birthdays	60
31.	Exclusion	62

32. In Winnipeg   64
33. Jackson   66
34. Jen's Birthday   69
35. On the Farm   71
36. Stereotypes   73
37. Garden Magic   75
38. Great Uncle Mike   77
39. Father's Day   79
40. Wasting Food   81
41. Larva   83
42. Not Random or Determined   85
43. Jackson's Baptism   87
44. Seventieth Birthday   89
45. Odds and Ends   92
46. Motorcycle   94
47. Nine-eleven   96
48. Becky's Birthday   98
49. Flickers   100
50. Andy's Birthday   102
51. Colorado Trip and Luke's Birthday   105
52. Aunt Agnes   107
53. Good News and Other News   109
54. October Thoughts   111
55. From Winona to Durian to…   113
56. Glaucoma   115
57. Thanksgiving   117
58. No Boring Days   119
59. Christmas   121
60. Thoughts of Jesus   123
61. Luke's Baptism   125
62. New Year's and Recycling   128
63. Triskaidekaphobia   130
64. Genome   132
65. Things that Can't be Bought   134
66. Food and Sacrament   136
67. Last Supper   138
68. Tragedy   140

69. Eats, Shoots and Leaves 142
70. Segways 144
71. Shrove Tuesday 146
72. Chaos 148
73. Unfairness 150
74. Reconciliation 152
75. San Diego Trip 154
76. Good News 157
77. Earth Day 159
78. Beautiful Hand 161
79. Grandpa's Sis Teresa 163
80. Nature's Magic 165
81. Robins 167
82. New Wheels 169
83. Breathe 171
84. Numinous Delights 173
85. More Odds and Ends 175
86. Autumn 177
87. Halloween 179
88. Sarah and Mike's Wedding 181
89. Gordo 184
90. Christmas in Rochester 186
91. Interesting Discoveries 188
92. Change and Aunt Mick 190
93. Cherokee Story 192
94. Beauty without Asking 194
95. We Had So Much Snow… 196
96. Magnificence 198
97. Cajuns 200
98. Stories of Events and Feelings 202
99. Bible Stories 204
100. Happy Easter 206
101. Easter Symbols 208
102. Wickedly Chocolate 210
103. Unwelcome Guest 213
104. Colorado Trip 215
105. Mother Nature 217

INTRODUCTION

May 13, 2007

Dear Grand Children,

These letters are for you, to stretch your awareness and imaginations, to recognize life as holy, and to make choices that bring healing to you and all Earthlings.

You are wonder-fully made, eternally loved, and destined to pursue the elusive Cosmic Dreamer who sets our world in motion with all the possibilities that life offers. All roads lead to the Divine; some of them are bumpy and full of potholes, others are scenic, and there may be many detours. You each decide your route, and there are many rest areas and visitor centers along the way. The letters will tell you about some of your relatives and the roads they chose.

Most of all, we write to tell you that you are treasured, needed, wanted, intriguing, creative, surprising, talented and inspiring, and that you always have a special place in our hearts.

With love to our Delightful Grand Children,

Grandma and Grandpa

1

Genesis

Nov 1, 2004

Dear Grand Children,

This is The Feast of All Saints, November 1, so this is a perfect day to write to you about how you are a part of God's beautiful creation. There are two Creation stories in the Bible, and many other creation stories told by other religions and cultures, all of them trying to explain how we appeared on Earth, or how on Earth we could have appeared on our own! (A little humor here; you are permitted to laugh.)

The Bible Creation story we all know very well is about Eve and the apple. Eve was tempted by a snake, and in the very early days of humans, the snake was a sacred symbol especially for women. Anyway, when God asked Adam why he was eating the apple, he replied, "Eve made me do it!" Now, how many of you would be able to get out of a tight spot with your mom or dad by saying "Joe made me do it," or "Patricia made me do it." How many of you could get away with that? I don't think so. This story of Creation may not have happened in this exact way but it certainly contains truth. How many times have we followed someone else's idea—like raiding the cookie jar—and then didn't want to take the blame for doing it when Mom finds out? For more of this story, see the Bible, Genesis, chapter 2.

In Genesis, chapter 1, another Creation story tells us that we are wonderfully made in God's image. God made heaven and earth; sun and moon; water and sky; and God saw that all of it was good. Besides that, God created every kind of plant and seed-bearing fruit trees, fish, birds, animals and creeping creatures and saw that it was good. And in God's image, God created man and woman and saw that it was *very* good. God blessed man and woman and left ALL the fruits to be food for them.

Of course, there is more to this story, and I am not sure whether God created in this order or what one day meant in God-time. But I can tell you that we were created as beautiful and forever loved by the Divine Spirit whose dreams enfold us with endless possibilities. See Genesis, chapter 1 in the bible.

So today, you can celebrate your uniqueness (you NEEK ness; it means no other person is like you) your talents and gifts, the way you see nature, and the way you recognize that you are loved and blessed by God.

Our love,

Grandma and Grandpa

2

At the Cottage

Nov 15, 2004

Dear Grand Children,

    We spent last weekend at your Aunt Becky and Uncle Mike's cottage on Silver Springs Lake. It is a season when Earth begins to take a rest from the prolific growing days of summer. The leaves have fallen and we chopped them up with the mower and left them on the grass to become compost. The soil is a sandy loam, so each year the leaves will enrich it for grass and plants.

    Bluebirds have made their home at the Lake, and we have watched Sandhill Cranes wander along the bank. Becky says Coyotes are in the area but we never have seen them. We have spied deer tracks in their yard, and I'm sure that if we were to look for them at dusk, we could observe them hunting for food in the woods close to the lake.

    Some of you are aware that Native Americans respected the animals and thought their animal cousins were so smart that the Natives followed them to find food and water. When they hunted animals for food, they also asked permission of the animal spirit. This awareness of animal spirit seems to be common among early peoples, those who lived in Africa and also those in Australia and New Zealand.

We are blessed to have abundant animal and plant life. It would be difficult to imagine life without them. They are *not* there for us *to use* as much as they are to give us delight, to show us beauty, to uncover other miracles of life, to overwhelm us with the abundance of earth, to reveal the Divine hand in all of creation, and to be inspired with gratitude for our Earth home. We need to take care of Earth and all that is in it and on it, because without each part that makes up our world, our lives would not be as *wonder-full.*

With love to you and your families,

Grandma and Grandpa

3

Thanksgiving

Nov 25, 2004

Dear Grand Children,

This Thanksgiving we have many things for which to be grateful. The word gratitude is from *gratus*, (now you know a Latin word) meaning precious, pleasing, full of favor, full of pleasing beauty or form, and grace.

Do you know you are wonderfully formed? If you haven't found that out yet, believe us that it's true! You are wonderfully formed and have the ability to jump, climb, sleep, rest, breathe, pump blood, move your head, see, hear, taste, touch, smell (well, most of the time what we smell is pleasing), and so many other things that you will not be able to think of all of them. We are thankful for you being wonderfully formed.

Do you know that your heart may reside in your body and pump blood to keep all parts alive, but it also miraculously can lead you to knowledge? You can know, have a sense, of what is good without knowing it in your minds. When you are small, you see a flower—and it can be tiny or large—and you know that it is beautiful. Only when you are older you might come to know it as a weed, so you have an advantage in knowing it before it is identified as a weed. We think with our minds and not our hearts when we don't find a "value" in that weed or when it becomes a nuisance to us. We are thankful that you see the wonder of Creation with your hearts.

You already know that you are unique. There is no one else exactly like you, - no one else looks like you, feels like you, thinks like you, learns like you, views things like you. The mysterious part of your uniqueness is that you can understand and appreciate other people because you know (in your heart?) that they have these unique qualities, too. All of Earth's living things are unique and our Creator keeps us spellbound with the diversity of it. We each—person, flower, bird, creature, blade of grass—carry a spark of Divine Life, and together we create an incomplete but beautiful picture of the Divine. We are thankful that you are unique.

And we are thankful for your parents, because without them, you wouldn't be here!

With gratitude for you,

Grandma and Grandpa

4

Advent

Dec 1, 2004

Dear Grand Children,

This is the time for you to be nice to your parents because they seem to have a direct line to Santa Claus! You may already have come to the same conclusion.

Santa helps us celebrate Christmas. Jesus was born, and so we have given gifts to each other as a sign of our "gratitude" for his life. When Jesus lived on earth, he taught us that we should take a look at our lives and figure out why we don't get along and why some of us are treated without respect. Then Jesus recommended that we begin to change so that we all live like we are brothers and sisters and belong to the family of God. You may turn up your noses to treating everyone as brother and sister, but I know in your hearts that you would defend your blood brother or sister if he or she were in trouble. To treat everyone as part of our family, we would have to be good listeners so that we could understand how the other person feels and thinks, and learn the other person's dreams and life story.

Jesus cared very much about his Jewish community. When he was living, the Romans occupied Jewish territory and forced the Jews to feed and house them and sometimes carry their weapons for them. Jesus knew that taking up weapons against the Romans would not free the Jews and would create more violence. Instead, he suggested that they find other ways to resist the Roman occupation, and he also recommended that they love their enemies. But that doesn't mean that Jesus thought the Jews should accept Roman disrespect; Jesus meant that treating others as the Jews wanted to be treated would bring a change in the Romans.

Here is a prayer we are using during this Advent/ Waiting season

> ADVENT PRAYER
> Holy and loving Creator,
> You fill our hearts with longing for simple things;
> with love and laughter, stories and dreams,
> refreshment and peace.
> You inspire us to be creators of justice
> and welcoming to all your family
> as we wait with green and growing hope
> to celebrate your coming.
> In gratitude we breathe in and out your love.
> Amen.

With love,

Grandma and Grandpa

5

Magic

Jan 2, 05

Dear Grand Children,

Rochester is magical today! Last evening we had rain and sleet, and this morning the sun is highlighting our frozen world, making our yard a land of gems. The gorgeous view of this magic can't be captured in a picture, but we tried it anyway.

The snow that fell just before Christmas is gone except for a small part of the sledding ramp that you created. We may get more snow this week with more delightful sights, and it could give us backaches, too, when we shovel it! Good things sometimes have undesirable consequences.

Have any of you made New Year's resolutions? We always make one or two; more than that would be too difficult to manage. Resolutions are made to improve our lives, or to restore some magic. Some people say that we are on Earth to learn about the magic of life, and once we are touched by it, we will thank our Creator. We will appreciate the wonders that surround us, and take care of ourselves and everything that we encounter in our lives. Sometimes that encounter feels like an intruder or an unwelcome guest, and sometimes we are very happy that it dropped in on us!

We know about the magic of children and grand children. You each are blessings from the Love and Light that made possible all of the marvelous creation surrounding us. Don't be afraid to look around, explore, try out, examine, listen, and taste. Sometimes you will make mistakes, but if you follow your intuition and the reminders of your parents, you can avoid wrong steps. Being an explorer is risky. Sometimes a person can fall off a mountain, or taste something that definitely resembles vinegar, but you know enough to consider the incline of the mountain or to smell before tasting a wee bit.

So, Magical Seekers, take on this year with a spirit of adventure but, *very important,* hang on to the safety cord of intuition and common sense, and consider what your parents might tell you in a new situation. There are many ways to add magic to your lives, so select the best for you.

For a magical 2005,

Grandma and Grandpa

6

Martin Luther King Day

Jan 20, 05

Dear Grand Children,

We remembered Martin Luther King last evening. We went to the Rochester Public Library—you all have been there—to watch a movie about a time in April, 1968, when Martin Luther King jr. helped the striking Memphis garbage haulers. The strike was about not having vacation time. It was about the puny (little) wages (money they earned for the work they did) for keeping Memphis clean and free of rats and other animals that love garbage. It was about cleaning up after other people, about being treated like the garbage they collected, and about wanting respect as members of the community where their work of collecting garbage was important to everyone.

Support for the garbage haulers came from the black community because most haulers were black. The white community usually didn't bother themselves about how the African-Americans lived, whether they had a paid vacation; whether their wages were enough to afford decent housing, food and clothes for their families. One of the garbage haulers said he would take off his shoes and overalls outside his door because he didn't want to bring maggots into his home. Maggots are soft, legless grubs that change into houseflies.

Martin Luther King spoke to the black community the night before the protest march. He ended his talk to them this way:

> Well, I don't know what will happen now. We've got some difficult days ahead But it doesn't matter with me now, because I've been to the mountaintop. And I don't mind. Like anybody, I would like to live a long

11

life. Longevity has its place. But I'm not concerned about that now. I just want to do God's will. And He's allowed me to go up to the mountain. And I've looked over. And I've seen the Promised Land. I may not get there with you. But I want you to know tonight, that we, as a people, will get to the Promised Land. And I'm happy, tonight. I'm not worried about anything. I'm not fearing any man. Mine eyes have seen the glory of the coming of the Lord.

The next morning, as he left the motel to join the marchers, he leaned down to a friend and requested a song to Sweet Jesus—his last words—and was killed, the victim of a sniper bullet.

We miss our brother, Dr. Martin Luther King, jr., because he was a leader who helped us all to overcome some economic and racist intolerance. He was a man who had to neglect his own family to do this work, and we realize that, like all of us, he was not perfect. But his compassion, nonviolent activism, and courage inspire us all.

With our love,

Grandma and Grandpa

7

Sarah's Birthday

Feb 5, 05

Dear Grand Children,

Today is your Aunt Sarah's birthday! She is thirty years young, but more than twice as old as any of you. Still, she is young and has lived in many different places, worked a variety of jobs, attended several schools and universities, and made many friends. All of this makes her an eclectic person, which means, from her large number of experiences she can select the best of all of them and have it benefit her life.

Since graduating from high school, Sarah has developed running and biking skills and recently entered fun racing events. She knows that she needs time and space to be alone. We all need this, but she has realized it sooner than most of us. She is smart enough to know when her lifestyle is not the best for her and then she is strong enough to change it. She is a talented artist, and not afraid to speak—to anyone—about her opinions and concerns. Her inquisitive and questioning mind directs her choices so that she avoids what does not seem authentic or true, even when it is not popular. This gift is recognized by others who search her out for conversations, and they become "soul" friends with her. She is fun to be with, and laughs easily.

More than this, she has style and class!

My favorite story about her happened during the time she struggled to keep a job and go to cosmetology school in Milwaukee. She was trying to balance her pay with her needs. She was always short on money then. As she waited at a traffic light one cold wintry day, a man dressed with worn clothes that were too thin for the weather was standing next to her. She glanced over, and seeing him shivering, she handed him her mittens, knowing he needed them more than she did.

That man would be called a street person, one who doesn't have a regular home or place to live. He might have become a street person because he was physically or mentally ill, or because he lost a job, or for any number of other reasons that you might try to imagine, but I'm sure he would tell you that he never intended to live on the streets. And I'm sure that he is a member of God's family. If you have some questions about this, we could think about them together.

We are grateful for Sarah's gifts and for her serendipitous friendships. Serendipitous (ser-an-DIP-it-us) means something good that we weren't searching for, something that happens without our wanting it, a happy event we didn't plan.

We all can appreciate Sarah's gifts, but we have them, too; generosity, inner strength, the ability to recognize the truth and act on it, and talents that we still are uncovering. And we have variety, our own style, and serendipity, too!

Love to the Birthday Girl and you Grand Children,

Grandma and Grandpa

8

Honeybees

Feb 6, 05

Dear Grand Children,

I caught a bug that I didn't want. It attacked on Wednesday, and made me nap away most of Thursday and Friday. It inflamed my throat, making it scratchy, and so I fought it with, would you guess, honey?

Recently I read that honey is good for healing an open wound, so I thought it might be good for healing an inner wound, too. I used a half teaspoon of honey and slowly swallowed it, hoping it would touch the places on my throat that felt raw. Rubbing Vicks on my neck also helped the soreness go away. So the next time you have a sore throat, or a tickle in your throat that makes you cough, ask your mother to give you some honey. It can't hurt you and it tastes yummy, but if you ask too often, she may think you are pretending to be sick!

Honey is a "mystic (mysterious) universe and the substance for divinity," according to one writer enthralled with this food that almost never goes stale.

New studies are being made about its use as a dressing for wounds and burns especially since bacteria are developing ways to fight antibiotics. Honey works well for people whose wounds are not healing with the usual ointments. Infections clear up faster, and new skin growth appears sooner with honey, and the best news for us is that there seems to be no bad side effects! This is in a study by Dr L.B. Grotte.

Today, some scientists claim that even though honey is sweet, if taken in the right dosage as a medicine, it does not harm diabetic patients. We know of people who use honey that is made from the plants and weeds in their own neighborhoods who believe that it helps

15

clear up their allergies. There is some proof that honey can control high blood pressure. Many other cures have been attributed to honey but not enough research has been done to prove the claims by people who are convinced that honey has helped their medical problems.

Just as important as the medicinal benefits of honey is the pollination that bees do for fruit and nut trees and blooming plants that give us beauty as well as food. One third of our crops are pollinated by bees! That's a lot of work they do for us! Without their help, our food supply would be scarce.

Bees are a delicate insect. It is really hard for a swarm of bees to find a new home. And bees have to watch out for bears and skunks that like to eat them. Once worker bees feel threatened by an animal or human, they sting for their own protection, but then their stingers get separated from them and they die.

Some people describe bees as industrious, cooperative, sweet, and reminders of the soul. Look for them in your neighborhoods and treat them well.

Love to our Honeys,

Grandma

9

Teresa's Birthday

Feb 7, 05

Dear Grand Children,

What do you dream for yourself? What are your aspirations (hopes)? Your parents and teachers and other important people in your lives have dreams for you, so you may find it difficult to dream beyond *their* wish list.

You might want good grades or want to be a starter on your athletic team, grow up to be a forest ranger or ship's captain, but we all know that it just doesn't happen by wishing for it. No, dreams are fun but to make them happen takes a lot of work, and even then it might not happen soon.

To ascend a ladder, one must climb every rung. To achieve good grades, one must take the steps; do the reading, finish homework and hand it in, listen in class, and study for tests. But there are distractions every day that entice one away, so, for some of us, the hardest "rung" of the ladder is keeping our eyes on that goal.

To keep that goal in sight, one must be able to get up from a fall, to go on in spite of disappointments, to have the courage and spunk and toughness to start again. It also helps to be stubborn! Stubbornness can be an asset (advantage). There is no time to feel sorry for yourself; if you have a goal that you want to achieve, you must get back on that ladder wherever you fell off.

Today we celebrate a beautiful 44 years with a beautiful person. She has achieved a masters degree, a perfect score on her math SAT (a test to qualify for college classes), proficiency in several musical instruments, and she is highly regarded for the work she does with the Manitoba government dealing with children's issues. As a runner, she won awards in high school and college, and became an international runner for Canada; ask her about her trips, especially to China. Incredible achievements and we didn't mention all of them! She finds her greatest satisfaction being a mom, enjoying her sons.

If you think it was easy for her, you would be wrong. She has had some major struggles and disappointments. Because of her dealing with these problems and from her experiences in overcoming them, she knows how to get back on that ladder and continue going forward. If ever you are feeling discouraged, disappointed, or don't know how to start again, you should visit with her. Happy birthday, Teresa.

With love to our adventurers,

Grandma and Grandpa

Chris and Teresa

Teresa and her sons,
Connor and Eamon

Kaylee & Shea, Chris's children

19

10

Lent and Spring

Feb 9, 05

Dear Grand Children,

At this time of year, nature seems to be asleep, and yet we begin to anticipate another spring when the daffodils and tulips peep through the snow to miraculously display their individual colors.

Is it a happy accident that followers of Jesus celebrate their greatest feast in the spring? Easter is determined by the season and the full moon, so the date changes each year. Some years we have snow, and sometimes we have more flowers blooming than tulips and daffodils.

When we were young, to prepare for Easter, we "gave up something" for Lent, which was the forty days before Easter. We would not eat candy or desserts. Adults might give up smoking or coffee. As we grew older, we were encouraged to "do something" for Lent,—read a few verses of the Bible, or visit someone who was sick.

These practices of "giving up something" and "doing something" continue to be good ways of exercising our mental muscles. The "giving up" can enhance our lives, make our families healthier, and get rid of a bad habit. The "doing something" is just another opportunity to form good habits. No one is sure about when or how these Lenten practices began except they show up in our history records about two hundred years after Jesus died.

We do know that spring was celebrated even before Jesus was born. Ancient religions of the Brits, Celts, Germans, Greeks, Mayans and Persians celebrated a god who overcame the powers of darkness. Some of them even had resurrection stories. This is not surprising because spring is a resurrection (coming alive again) with new green growing things. We watch this cycle of renewal as Mother Earth awakens from her winter sleep and once again reveals her astounding gifts for all of us to share. For us, the Lenten practices are a way to re-vitalize (give new life) and restore (make new and healthy again).

Nature has many doorways that allow us to glimpse the Divine Creator. It happens when our spirits and bodies are nourished by the beauty of our part of the world. Then our hearts and minds hum a tune of gratitude for the world's magical garden that is our home. We happily await another spring but right now Nature is blanketing us with snow!

Love to our Hearts' Delights,

Grandma and Grandpa

11

St. Valentines

Feb 14, 05

Dear Grand Children,

Enjoy St. Valentine's Day, a time for girls to talk sweetly to boys and for boys to be especially nice to girls! Wait! Read on!

St. Valentine lived so many years ago that we don't have any good records of who he was. In fact, three people have had that name, and all may have been special persons. In 1969, the Church decided not to celebrate this feast because not enough was known about the saint who was named Valentine.

You may be surprised to learn that the roots of this celebration of Valentines Day come from an ancient Roman festival to honor the god Lupercus which was on February 15. It was an important day for Roman men because they were seeking the "affections of women." Not only that, but in the fourteenth and fifteenth centuries, many people thought that birds chose their partners in the middle of February. Do you think that is when the term "love birds" began? I can tell you that at Silver Lake Park in Rochester, we have noticed the ducks and geese pairing up!

Well, those people who lived hundreds of years ago thought of love when they noticed birds mating, and wrote letters and sent small gifts to their Sweethearts. It doesn't matter whether birds mate in the middle of February or even whether St. Valentine lived. What matters is that we have another day to celebrate each other on February 14.

We celebrate you today by breathing special thoughts of happiness and peace. We breathe you love to warm your hearts and minds, music to fill your souls. We breathe you a mountain of surprises to fill your world, dance to drench your playful spirits.

As you breathe in and out, send peace and love to your families and friends. And then breathe peace and love to our distant relatives across the oceans, and to our brothers and sisters who have authority and power over many people. Breathe blessings to our four-legged and winged cousins. You make a difference for all of us who live in our Earth Garden. If a flock of butterflies in Asia can determine the air currents in our country, we know you have at least that much power!

We breathe love and peace to our Grand Valentines,

Grandma and Grandpa

12

Eagle Watching

Feb 17, 05

Dear Grand Children,

Yesterday we met your great-aunt and great-uncle Mary and Bill Jenney in Red Wing. We spent some time along the Mississippi River at a place where an electric company cools its equipment with water from the river. Then that water is pumped back into the river warmer than it was before. Because of that, the river doesn't freeze in that area and becomes a good place for birds to nest in winter because of plentiful running water. We saw ducks, crows, and hundreds of Eagles!

Did you know that if your mom or dad would lie down flat on the ground, the eagle could spread its wings and cover them? They are humongous birds! After five years their white heads and tails tell us they have become adults. They soar above the water looking for something to eat, and then with a twist of their wings, can change direction or manage a slow glide. The crows were able to maneuver in the wind, but the ducks had to flap furiously to make any headway.

Eagles build their nests to accommodate one or two eaglets along with the parents. Nests can get as big as seven feet across, longer than your bed. On a website we watched Eagles build a nest, saw a two-month-old Eaglet, a fledgling, experimenting with flapping its wings and then trying to figure out how to fold them back up!

These amazing and beautiful birds roost in large trees along the river, and you can spot them easily because of their white markings. They eat fish dead or alive, and munch on mice and other rodents. A few years ago, Eagles were an endangered species; there were so few that they may not have survived. Certain pesticides were banned and now the eagles are more numerous.

We appreciate our winged cousin Eagle and its magnificent soaring ability, applaud its tidying up by eating rodents and dead fish, and laugh at the hilarious fledgling that doesn't know how to use its wings! And the Creator of all things smiles as we marvel at our Earth Home.

With love to you and with gratitude for your parents,

Grandma and Grandpa

13

Enchanting Sunday

Feb 20, 05

Dear Grand Children,

Winter is working her magic in Rochester again, and has dressed the outdoors in a heavy, furry mantle. Our large pine tree in the back yard is bowing with the creative work of our weather, its lowest branches brushing the white ground. And it continues to snow! We are at six inches and heading for a possible ten inches by this evening.

We were playing in the snow this morning, trying to find our driveway, and marveling at the white sparkling gems.

Squirrels have their highway systems on the power wires and along the fence tops. Today, they get three or four steps away from a tree, can't manage to move in the snow, and climb back into the safety of the limbs. After other snowfalls that haven't been this deep, they travel on the ground, and scurry as fast as they can over the top of the snow; every three or four steps they fall through, and then scramble to run over the top of the snow pack again. Can you imagine them being surprised when they fall into the snow? No wonder they like the power wires.

Today we are thankful for our warm house and the food we have stored away, like the squirrels, so that we don't have to travel in this snow to buy more. We often don't think about the numbers of people it takes to grow our food, process it and package it, transport it to the store, have someone stack it on shelves, and then all we have to do is go around with our carts and make our choices. When you think about what goes into a loaf of bread,—planting the grain, harvesting, grinding the grain at a mill, adding yeast and other ingredients and letting it rise and bake at the bakery, and then packaging it,—that bread is inexpensive! We are fortunate for the many reliable people working to provide us with food.

We are grateful for today's beauty, that we have a warm place to live, and that we have an abundance of food. We are grateful for the amusing squirrels and their lithe and flexible maneuvers. We are grateful for responsible people who work at jobs to provide us with food so that we don't have to plant and harvest it by ourselves. We are grateful for your parents who work to provide for you; our parents cared for us in this way, too. As our hearts sing with gratitude for this enchanting Sunday, we invite you to join us in thanking our Creator for these blessings.

Love to you on this enchanting Sunday,

Grandma and Grandpa

14

Violence in School

Feb 22, 05

Dear Grand Children,

Do you enjoy going to school? Is it a pleasant place, even though you may have to study and work hard to understand some of your subjects? Is it a safe place?

Last week we read about a middle school where children fought, and even the girls were getting physically mean. This school decided to do something about it. Each week, they have two home-room classes to talk about fairness or about what happened at school during that week. Sometimes they have a video that portrays cultural differences or that demonstrates a good character trait,—courage, accepting others, being a peacemaker, welcoming others, using kind words, respecting others. It also is an opportunity for the students to share their life stories with each other.

Already the school is becoming more calm and serene, and the students are being more accepting of others. It tells us that education is more than studying class subjects. Education includes knowing how to treat others. We all need to work on respecting others and understanding cultural differences. When we respect other people and accept other cultures, we open ourselves to more friendships and more ways of celebrating life, and that is a welcome discovery.

In this adventure called life, we learn to accept others and to make peace with those who solve their problems in a different way than we would choose. We won't always know the outcomes when we reach out to others, all of them members of God's family. *We don't have to know the outcomes*, because we are treating our global family members the way we would like to be treated. When we respect others, we give them a chance to feel good about themselves, and because of our example they may give others that same respect.

You already are accepting others, respecting them and using kind words. You are being a peacemaker when you listen to them and show them that you care about them. You are learning how to make your school and neighborhood a better place for everyone when you breathe peace. You are changing the world!

Peace, blessings and love,

Grandma and Grandpa

15

Uncle Joe's Birthday

Feb 23, 05

Dear Grand Children,

When we were in grade school, we sometimes had two school holidays in February, one on the 12th for Abe Lincoln's birthday and one on the 22nd for George Washington's birthday. If your Uncle Joe had been born on the 22nd, his name might be George. I wonder, is he happy or sad that he wasn't given that name?

Joe's life has been full of wonderful experiences,—in high school his bike trip to the Black Hills, his work at a bike shop, evening janitor, and setting up TVs at St. Mary's Hospital. Now the hospital has a TV in every room, but when he worked there, when patients requested TV, he would roll one to their rooms and hook it up to cable. In high school he was a member of the dance band, and had the lead in the musical "Charlie Brown" which made us very nervous because we didn't know he could sing.

He used his carpentry and electrical skills working in theaters in high school and college. His handiwork is evident everywhere he has lived. He made the most of his education at Marquette, and participated in the coed intramural sports, learning many new skills. He took up wind-surfing and sailing. His latest adventure is this month of study in Washington DC, where he is learning negotiation strategies.

Experiences like these are possible if you have the courage to try new adventures and if you are willing to take on a challenge. It is gutsy to try something that others think is too different or weird or not cool or not popular. His bike trip took effort and stamina that others would not think of doing. That was a trip of discovery, sleeping in a tent or in a church and meeting unique people. He has many stories to tell about that trip, so ask him about it sometime.

He has had disappointments but that hasn't dampened his courage or stopped him from accepting new challenges. He has discovered ways to solve his problems by looking at all his choices; sometimes he has chosen the difficult but correct choice, and that requires courage. He is able to be thankful in spite of the disappointments. *Being thankful is a huge blessing because it heals the sadness in our lives.*

Joe dreams of something better than what is, and he works to make it happen. He is an enthusiastic participant in sports, an artist, an appreciated worker in his office, a good cook, and most of all, a dedicated Dad. Talk with him when you have a challenge or need someone to boost your courage.

Love to our Courageous Ones,

Grandma and Grandpa

16

Precious Earth

Feb 26, 05

Dear Grand Children,

We are a part of what makes Earth tick, and I don't mean wood ticks. I mean tick, like our heart-beats, like an easy-pedaling smooth-running bicycle. In order for the heart to work well, we eat healthy foods and give it some exercise. For a bike to work well, we clean it up and oil it and after we use it, set it down or use a kick-stand instead of dropping it to the ground.

Earth is in a dangerous situation today. She is losing some of her beautiful creatures,—the Carolina parakeet, the Passenger Pigeon, the Blue Pike, a plant that used to grow in Kentucky and Indiana called the Bigleaf Scurfpea, a Tennessee clam, and the Eastern Elk. They are extinct, meaning they no longer exist on Earth. More creatures than this have become extinct.

The Blue Pike became extinct after being over-fished to sell at supermarkets, and after we unknowingly poisoned their water which destroyed their habitat. When we began using our rivers and lakes as dumps, we didn't think about how it would affect the water and all the fish and other living things that relied on that water. When our fish became scarce, we knew something was wrong. We didn't realize that our actions could be so damaging to our Earth Home. Now we have to find new ways of getting rid of our garbage to save Earth.

Some of you have been to Duluth, Minnesota. This city has a plan for creating ponds to collect rainwater. The first of these ponds will filter out some of the dirt from city streets. Then the water will go through a wetland (swampy) area with plants which take out some of the pollutants (poisons). Pollutants can come from garden and insect sprays that are rinsed out of the soil by the rainwater. Artists have created some interesting sculpture designs called flowforms that will purify the water even more. The water then will travel to large basins where it swirls, generating enough motion for the water to oxygenate (take a bath in oxygen. I don't recommend that you take an oxygen bath, though.) This has been in the planning stage for a long time, but I can imagine that we will see all this soon in downtown Duluth by strolling the walkways along the waterfront.

We need clean water and good food to nourish us, the four-leggeds and winged creatures to inspire us. Our life is connected with everything in the Universe. The Universe is our way of seeing and knowing and talking to the Divine. When we observe the Universe, we make a connection with the Cosmic Dreamer. When we walk on Earth, we walk on holy ground. Let's listen to Earth's sighs and dreams so she can direct us in caring for her.

With love to our Treasures,

Grandma and Grandpa

17

Earthlings

Feb 28, 05

Dear Grand Children,

Do you enjoy science? The mystery of it? Life is experienced by every creature in a variety of ways. Humans live on planet Earth with species of plants and animals.

How are we different from other species on Earth? We can express how enthralled and charmed we are to live in the beauty of our Earth Home. But other species have a way of communicating, too. We remember things, and so do our four legged cousins. We feel, and so do our plant relatives.

At one time we were taught that there are living things that change and non-living things that don't. But there is a problem with this. In California, you feel Earth tremble when she shifts her position. The bottom of the ocean also rumbles with change and creates new islands. Leaves decompose. Can you think of something that doesn't change?

Another mystery is how we have the same elements as Earth. We are about 71% water and so is Earth. As you eat a banana, think about how that banana came to be. The plant was grown in soil, fed by the sun, and watered by the rain. We eat the banana, so we take in all those elements from Earth. Bananas contain iron, zinc, manganese, sodium, potassium, calcium, magnesium, and copper! It has the same elements as soil, but you probably would prefer eating those elements in a banana rather than in a dish of soil.

We know that the sun, soil, and water work their magic on the banana plant so that the same elements arrange themselves in a way to create the banana, just as we eat the banana which becomes part of us. That is a mystery! Each species seems to be programmed to combine the elements found on Earth into creating themselves again and again. Within the human species we are related because we have the same combination of elements, yet there is such a variety that each person is unique. What a beautiful display of creativity!

Here's another thought for you. The four-leggeds and winged creatures eat from the same plants and trees and animals. Their elements are the same as ours, too; each species is programmed to combine the food they eat into creating themselves again and again. Yet, if you look at the squirrels playing in your yard, you will notice that they have different personalities, so they are unique. The same elements that determine us as humans are the same ones that determine the animals' species, so that makes them our cousins. And Earth is our Mother!

Peace and love to our Earthlings,

Grandma and Grandpa

18

Rediscover our Unity

Mar 1, 05

Dear Grand Children,

You are caught in a great re-discovery! It is a re-discovery because the human species once knew in their hearts about how they relied on plants and animals and Mother Earth for their lives, and now we are learning this again.

We lost that sense knowing where we fit in the Universe when we thought we could manipulate and control everything around us. Our ancestors worked very long and hard to clear the land for crops. They invented machines to help us pull, push, transport, dig, weave, keep cool, and make hot. They discovered oil and devised ways of using it for energy. They did all of this to make our lives easier and wonderful.

Now we realize that all things work together. One example; by using gas, oil and coal for energy, we release carbon into the air. Carbon itself is not the problem. Trees and plants need carbon to grow, but we are releasing more than our plants can use. This problem still needs to be solved. We could make our cars and other vehicles more efficient so that they use less gas, and we could use more wind and air power; eventually we will need to think of other sources of energy because gas, oil and coal are not renewable resources.

So we are beginning to realize we know very little about how everything works together. One of the best ways of taking care of our Earth Home is by respecting everything in it and on it.

One thousand years ago, a Chinese official had an inscription on his wall that said, "The dome of the sky is my father and Earth is my mother and even such a small creature as I have an intimate (close) place in its midst. All that is in the universe and which directs the universe is also within me. All people are my brothers and sisters and all things are my companions." Many years ago, our ancestors had a respect for Earth and the Universe, as you can tell by that quote.

You are experiencing the changing attitudes toward Earth, respecting and caring for her instead of using everything as if there will be more for ever and ever. You may be recycling paper, tin, aluminum, and plastic at home and school. That helps. Some of you may dream or discover ways to restore Earth to a healthy home. One man discovered that mushrooms help to clean up polluted wetlands.

This is an exciting and dangerous time to live, exciting because of all the possible ways we can heal our Earth Home, and dangerous because we need to do it so that we and our four-legged and winged cousins and plant relatives can live in harmony.

Love to our Blessed Grand Dreamers,

Grandma and Grandpa

19

Ben's Birthday

Mar 4, 05

Dear Grand Children,

Ben is the youngest of your Mayer aunts and uncles, and is closer in age to some of his nieces and nephews than to some of his brother and sisters. Like you, he is observing and discovering the world and learning his place within it.

When he was about four years old, Ben would watch the TV artist with his mother. The artist called most everything beautiful—the colors he used, the scene he was painting, the day even when it rained. Ben encouraged his mother to paint, and so she did.

He walked with his mother to St Pius School for kindergarten, just a little more than a mile from home. One day when Ben decided he didn't want to go to school, he hid under the bed. He rolled away from his mother who tried to pull him out, but she didn't fit underneath far enough to catch him. So she called his dad to come home from work to help her. Ben never tried it again because he knew it wouldn't work.

When Ben was in junior high, he taught his mom and dad how to use the computer. Whenever we had a problem with it, we would go to him. When he first started using the computer, there was no "Windows" program, and one of his Science Fair projects was to create an educational game, a feat that still has his parents baffled!

Ben is sorting through his educational and life experiences that have taught him about the world around him. He is "weeding out" the things that don't seem genuine for him. He is not dazzled by a lot of money or a lot of things. He finds creativity and beauty in his culinary (cooking) ability. Some of his other talents, his math ability and his capacity to solve all kinds of problems, are available for him whenever he chooses to use them. He is on a quest, a journey, to find out what is important for him and what inspires his life.

He is a blessing to us. His imagination, affection, intelligence, generosity and humor are needed by all of us here on this Earth Home.

He is not the only Ben Mayer. Another man with his name was a member of the Polaris Observatory Association, and a star is named after him; you can see his work if you search on your computer by using Ben Mayer Polaris. How cool is that?

We love you,

Grandma and Grandpa

20

Mary's Birthday

Mar 12, 05

Dear Grand Children,

This is your great-grandmother Marie Mayer's birthday. She was a hard-working love-filled lady, a math whiz and a doting grandmother. She shared her birth date with Mary Beth Mayer Weidner, but that didn't make Mary Beth any more special because everyone was special to Marie. Mary Beth is relieved to have a different last name because she thought her parents could have chosen a better first name to go with Mayer. When you say Mary Mayer out loud several times, it is a tongue-twister! The Beth in her name was supposed to solve that problem, but it was soon dropped by everyone. In fact, some of her friends called her Mare (like the old gray mare), so her name became Mare Mayer, and then shortened to Mare Mare.

Mary Beth has a great imagination. She became a teacher, maybe because she liked to play, enjoyed learning new things, had fun with children, and relished dressing up in costumes and funky duds. You need imagination to teach a class of 20 or more children with different ways of learning and having fun. On her first day of teaching, she lined up her grade-school pictures, and her class could see that she had a mischievous smile and wild hair and turned-up collars and a toothless grin, all part of accepting your own life and laughing at yourself.

Even though she no longer teaches, she organizes events at John Christopher and Ellie's school, and is a room mother, setting up a schedule for other volunteer mothers. Using her organizing skills, Mary Beth started a book club for women in her neighborhood and a children's play group. John and Ellie have had some merry (not Mary) birthday parties organized by their mother.

If you like adventure, she has some great stories to tell about an aviation class she took one summer. She has run a marathon, and participated in triathlons (a three-event race of running, swimming, and biking). She now teaches her children about the wonder of Monarch Butterflies and other nature mysteries, about the adventure you find in books, and about setting creativity free with arts and craft tools.

Mary Beth has a happy spirit and laughs with people. She is ready to take on new adventures. She has learned to relax rather than stress out on things that happen. She accepts that life is a journey, an adventure in finding the wonder that appears to us every day in the ordinary events, and she knows that *the journey is one of progress rather than perfection*. We are thankful for her imaginative and lively spirit.

Love to all our Grand Wondrous Children,

Grandma and Grandpa

Mary and John, Ellie in the backpack, and John Christopher

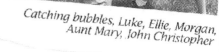

On the Mississippi

Catching bubbles, Luke, Ellie, Morgan,
Aunt Mary, John Christopher

Fun with a pinata

42

21

San Diego

Mar 13, 05

Dear Grand Children,

We have some good news and some bad news from San Diego. Our Grand Children, palm trees, and the weather are all pleasant and beautiful. The bad news is that Uncle Joe fractured his ankle in a roller hockey game on Monday night. He is in a "boot," keeping his foot elevated, and the physical shock is making him tired so he often drops off to sleep.

Before that happened, though, we spent several hours at our favorite place, Balboa Park. A glassblower was showing someone how to make vases. He is an artist, able to imagine how much air to breathe into the long metal tube with the pliable hot bulb of glass at the other end. This method was first used for making glass bottles by the Phoenicians before Jesus was born. Since then, many artists have experimented with using colors and designs for dishes, vases, and decorative pieces. This glassblower has awesome talent.

The flower pavilion at Balboa had orchids among the palm trees, water lilies in the ponds. Everywhere on the grounds are the Birds of Paradise, a bush with showy blooms that say "See how Beautiful I am!" It is called Bird of Paradise because the flower resembles a bird's beak and head feathers. The leaves are a larger version of the long and slender iris or daylily leaf, and the plant adds visual beauty wherever it is grown. It does not like to get cold, so it would refuse to grow in the Midwest.

Birds in San Diego resemble their Minnesota cousins. We have seen a few crows, which are obnoxious and clever at the same time. Like people, they enjoy green lawns, watermelons, fatty foods, and they are chatty with their families and neighbors. They also like rodents—which is a good thing,—and rob the nests of songbirds which is bad. Some birdwatchers claim that they put nuts on the road for cars to run over. They also use sticks and rocks to forage for their meals. But you can imagine what a "murder"—a flock of crows—can do to yards and sidewalks since they don't carry around porta-potties.

We made orangeade and lemonade from the fruit trees in Uncle Joe's back yard, a real treat and easy with an electric juicer!

Lemonade

1/4 cup of lemon juice
1/2 cup of sugar
Add enough water to make four cups.
Add more juice or sugar to suit your taste.
If you put it in the freezer for awhile, you can make a slushy.

Joe has a house-mate named Jerry. He is from Joe's old neighborhood, and has two young daughters who were with their Dad much of the time while we were there. JD likes to play TV games with them.

Plants are in bloom, although most of the deciduous trees are resting. Grass has to be tough to survive the sandy soil, and it requires lots of care. Snails, big and small, like his yard. They are ever-present in San Diego. I don't know whether snails are considered a nuisance, but they must be part of the life cycle in San Diego.

How fortunate that we could visit our family again, and in beautiful San Diego!

Love to all our Grand Ones,

Grandma and Grandpa

22

Leprechauns and St Patrick

Mar 17, 05

Dear Grand Children,

If only we could catch a leprechaun! We have heard that these wee creatures with wrinkled faces especially seem to enjoy Ireland. Living in farmhouses or wine cellars, they cobble (make) shoes, but only one of each type of shoe. Are leprechauns joking by making just one of each type of shoe?

The rumor is that they sometimes help us humans, and those who catch a leprechaun may be able to put their hands on the "pot of gold" that the wee ones possess. This pot of gold is hidden in secret places where only the leprechauns can reach, and sometimes it is at the end of a rainbow. If you are lucky enough to capture a leprechaun, he most likely will promise you the pot of gold if you let him go free. The only trouble with this is that if you blink or take your eyes off him for only a second, the leprechaun will disappear! Although it would be fun to have a leprechaun help us out, it may be more work to capture him and keep an eye on him than to do our own work!

Well, this is St. Patrick's Day, and the Irish are very proud of their special saint, and they should be. St. Patrick may not have been Irish, and he may not have used the shamrock to demonstrate how there can be three persons in one God. And all that doesn't matter; even the mystery of the Trinity doesn't matter.

What is important is that when St. Patrick lived among the Celts, he introduced them to the teachings of Jesus, and that enriched their spiritual lives. They hadn't known about Jesus, yet they believed that God was everywhere and that they could know God through the forest, hills, sky, sea, and all things in nature.

Places where people can feel a close connection to God are called "thin places." Ireland has many thin places, both natural ones and those made by people, where this close connection with God can be felt. One special place in Ireland, a burial tomb, was constructed even before the pyramids were built and before Jesus lived. Every year on December 21, this tomb has an opening that allows light inside for 17 minutes. People flock to see this. It reminds them that summer will come again and that there is life after death. So you can see that learning about Jesus made their belief stronger because St. Patrick told them about God's kingdom which is here in the magnificent universe, and about life beyond death.

For some Irish things to do, search the internet by typing in Irish fun for children.

With love to our Wee Ones,

Grandma and Grandpa

23

Wedding

Mar 22, 05

Dear Grand Children,

  You have a new uncle and two new cousins, but Connor and Eamon call them stepfather, stepsister and stepbrother! Yesterday Teresa and her very special friend Chris were married. The word, marry, means to blend, or to unite. So they promised to love and cherish each other for the rest of their lives. Chris has two children who are in high school, Shea and Kaylee. We hope that soon you will be able to meet them.

  For Teresa and Chris' wedding, we sent them this reflection.

  SPIRIT OF THE UNIVERSE, you have blessed Teresa and Chris with life, energy, good health, inquisitive minds, and the delight of love.

  They are your Creation and you call them by name from the beginning of time. Your magnificent weavings brought them into your scheme of the Universe. Your Wisdom connected them to the four-leggeds and winged creatures, and to all wondrous budding plants. Your imagination and abundance generated their inclusion in the intimate family and in the global family.

  They bless each other as they share their knowledge, gratitude, generosity and gifts, all blessings bestowed by their attachment to the Universe in which you are known.

  Joy is theirs as they marvel at Creation.

  Serenity is theirs as they embrace their lives.

  Humor is theirs as they contemplate mystery.

  Forgiveness is theirs as they unwrap their own holiness.

  Love endures as they walk side by side.

We join with Chris and Teresa in the celebration of their union as they are washed with your blessings that cannot be contained. We bow our heads and bend our knees as we are overcome with the lavishness of your Universe.

You can send them your good wishes and thoughts, too. Just breathe them in and out, and you will bless them and us as well. When you wish good thoughts to one person or two persons, those good thoughts overflow and touch others. Thank you!

Our love,

Grandma and Grandpa

24

Easter Thoughts

Mar 27, 05

Dear Grand Children,

Happy Easter! We are sure the Easter Bunny was generous to you, and we hope you stopped eating all the sweets before you had a sugar overdose!

We have never heard of an overdose of hard-boiled dyed eggs, another tradition of this feast. Ancient civilizations thought that the egg was the secret of new life. Ancient people who lived in India thought the world began when a humongous egg was split, one part becoming Earth and the other part becoming the heavens.

Early Christians used the egg, too, as a sign of new life. At Easter time we celebrate the change we will experience when we "die" and are "reborn" to new life. We remember that Jesus died and rose from the dead.

Christians are not the only people who celebrate life after death. Native Americans bury their dead friends and relatives with food, a fire-starting kit, and sometimes eating utensils for their journey to the spirit world. If they use caskets today, they drill a hole in it so the spirit can enter and leave freely. In their tradition, pipes, drums and rattles are used to help the departing soul on the journey. Sometimes they sing instructions and burn sage to help them get rid of anger and sadness. Burning sage, with its smoke and scent, also reminds them that their beloved friend or relative is taking a journey.

In the Jesus tradition, incense is burned to help the spirit rise to new life. Both incense and sage are ways of visualizing (seeing and sensing) what happens to the person who is passing on to new life.

Easter makes us think of new life in another way, too. We all are *becoming* new persons every day. We remember how we were yesterday and some of us remember how we were years ago. But every day is new, with new challenges, new opportunities, new adventures, new decisions. We discover something new every day about the great variety that fills our lives. We observe the world and see ourselves as part of the wondrous beauty of the Universe, and we are thankful for it. We breathe in and out the life-renewing air that surrounds us all in such holy magnificence.

Love to all you Breathing Beauties,

Grandma and Grandpa

25

Tsunami

April 10, 05

Dear Grand Children,

Tsunami. It is a Japanese word for a huge ocean wave caused by an earthquake or volcanic eruption which occurs at the bottom of the sea. It is a tidal wave. The worst tsunami we can remember happened the day after Christmas, in the ocean near the Indonesian Islands.

Just before the tsunami, the elephants were restless, trumpeting loudly and thundering up hills to higher ground. Crickets didn't sing. Dolphins swam to deeper water.

One group of Indonesians, who live on boats and are nomads on the water around these islands, noticed the change in the animals. They saw the water receding from land, making a large beach. One of the elders warned the others of his observations, and they either ran for higher ground or took their boats into deep water, imitating the animals. They survived the tsunami.

These Indonesians learn to swim before they can walk. Underwater, they look like tadpoles! Accustomed to the cold water, their heart rates are slower, and because of that they can hold their breath underwater longer than most people. They don't know how old they are because to them, time doesn't matter. Their relatives who live on the islands come to visit them, but the boat dwellers couldn't tell you whether they last visited five weeks ago or five years ago.

These indigenous people also don't have a word in their vocabulary for "want." They don't like to have a lot of things because they live in a boat. They have a word for "take," which means they know how to get what they need to live. One old man decided to go fishing for his breakfast. With his spear made from a tree branch with a small two-pronged end, he caught his fish in one try, and it was a big one.

When the tsunami devastated so much land and took many lives around Asia that day, some people explained it as punishment for something the Asians did wrong. But to the indigenous people, the tidal wave was just part of life. Like our ancestors, they knew how to watch animals for these signs. Most of us have lost that ability, but we can again learn to observe nature.

Remember, the Spirit of the Universe has given us a magnificent world to enthrall us and astonish us with its splendor. We never have to fear the anger of God because we are family to the Creator who loves us more than we can imagine. Breathe in God's peace and breathe it out to our Global family, Grand ones.

With love,

Grandma and Grandpa

26

Wakanhezas

May 1, 05

Dear Grand Children,

   You just heard about two new cousins when Teresa married her very special friend, Chris. His two children, Shea and Kaylee, are the newest cousins even though they are in high school.

   This summer you will be graced with two more cousins. One will have Mike and Becky for parents, and the other will join the family of Jen, Lee and Morgan. Parents anticipate this new Blessing and Wonder. A child can resemble his parents and sometimes their mannerisms. We can say that a child has certain gifts and talents that may seem to run in families. But each of us is so unique that not everything can be explained by the parents we have or the environment in which we live. We are mysteries!

   People from other cultures knew that their children were special, too.

   The Dakota Native American tribe uses the word "Wakanheza" for child, which also means 'sacred being'. "Wakanheza" explains a spiritual idea of the Dakota tribe—"that which is sacred is to be cherished, honored and respected."

   When a child is born into the Omaha Indian tribe, they announce "into your midst has come a new life" to the sun, moon, stars and everything in the universe. They ask to "make its path smooth, that it may reach the brow of the first hill." Then they pray the same way to the winds, clouds, rain, mist and all that moves in the air. They speak to the hills, valleys, rivers, lakes, trees, and grasses. Finally, they say, "Birds, great and small, that fly through the air; animals, great and small, that dwell in the forest; insects that creep among the grasses and burrow in the ground, hear me. Make this newborn's path smooth so that it can travel beyond the four hills." The "four hills" means the heavens, the atmospheric world, the earth and the animal kingdom. The Omaha tribe is asking the Universe, which is our clearest way of knowing God, to bring goodness and blessings to the new baby.

African tribes did a similar thing when a baby was born. Taking the baby to the highest hill, they raised it up for the whole universe to see and bless. What a wonderful way to celebrate a new life.

We anticipate, with amazement and delight the miracles of life coming this summer that will enrich all of us.

Love to our Wakanhezas,

Grandma and Grandpa

27

Snow and Creative Juices

May 2, 05

Dear Grand Children,

Nature played a joke on us during the night. All the roofs in Rochester were covered with snow, and this is May 2!!! Most of the snow on the ground melted soon after it fell, but the gardens were reluctant to part with its white outline and cover. Springtime will come again, but for now sitting outside in the sun with a good book to read is just a dream.

Last weekend, St. Pius Grade School performed *The Seussical*, a fun musical with speaking parts in rhyme, like the Dr. Seuss stories. The costumes were fabulous, the children performed with great confidence, and the audiences stood and clapped to show their appreciation. Grandma and another woman played the music for it with electronic pianos. Electronic pianos can make different sounds,—violins, organ, bass, brass, and vibes—and all were used at different times to enhance the music.

Music, a form of art, is a way to celebrate life, and that is one reason it is fun to participate in musical performances. Art is any form of creative work—drawing, building, dancing, gardening, and you might be able to think of other kinds of art. It is one of the most important parts of our lives.

In yesterday's paper, Marilyn vos Savant wrote that creative people are irreplaceable and more responsible for the advancement of our lives than philosophers and mathematicians. The groups who help us with improving our lives are the engineers, the builders. But it takes imagination to dream and create, and art of every kind to beautify our lives.

You know, too, that our family oozes with creative juices, and we know that all families have this creativity if they think about it. We all have been blessed with this attraction to immerse ourselves in music, art, drama, inventing, writing, and dance that enhance our lives for ourselves and everyone around us. Our world is brimming over with variety that feeds our imaginations. Plants and animals and birds and sunsets and moonscapes all say "look at me; look at me!" This Universe in its splendid array invites our senses to come to life. We are a part of a holy world that reflects the Cosmic Dreamer dwelling within everything. No wonder we want to dance and sing!

Love to our Creative Dreamers,

Grandma and Grandpa

28

Family Excursions

May 6, 05

Dear Grand Children,

We have had two family excursions since we last wrote. A few weeks ago, Grandma's sister Carolyn and her brother Mike, along with some of their family members, met for a game of baseball and supper at the Weidner's home. Children your age were there, and you may never have met them, but they are related to you. It is difficult to gather as a family because we have become larger. Children grow up, get married and have children of their own. And then you have the same thing with Grandpa's side of the family. To make your relatives even more numerous, you have another set of grandparents!

Yesterday we came home from a Cinco de Mayo celebration with Grandpa's side of the family. For supper we had tacos with refried beans prepared the way it is done in Guatemala by Martin (pronounced Mar TEEN in Spanish) who married into our family. He and his wife Barbara have adopted two children with Guatemalan ancestry who can speak Spanish. Their names are Jorge and Mercedes (Sadie). Although they are not blood relatives, they are members of our family *by choice*. And so our family grows!

Grandpa's side of the family will be celebrating a wedding July 16 in Iowa. Relatives from Omaha, Rochester and the Minneapolis area will drive to Waterloo to offer their best wishes and blessings for this marriage. They represent just a small part of your Mayer relatives but they carry the blessings of every member for the marrying couple. Our family connections are snaking across America!

Love to our Family-Rich Grand Children,

Grandma and Grandpa

29

Mother's Day

May 8, 05

Dear Grand Children,
   You may be surprised to learn that Mother's Day is an old custom beginning over 2000 years ago! The Greeks had a Spring Festival dedicated to Rhea, the mother of many gods, and the ancient Romans had a similar festival for their goddess-mother Cybele. Then Christians began to celebrate the fourth Sunday of Lent to honor Mary, the mother of Jesus. In England, this Sunday was expanded to include all mothers, and was called Mothering Sunday.
   Ann Jarvis, who lived in the Appalachian Mountains nearly 150 years ago, organized "mother's work day" to bring women together to speak out about poor health conditions in their community. She thought that women would be most concerned about this issue.
   In 1870, Julia Ward Howe, who promoted world peace and a woman's right to vote, organized a day "encouraging mothers to rally for peace." She wrote:

> Arise, all women who have hearts! We, the women of
> one country,
> Will be too tender of those of another country to allow
> our sons to be trained to injure theirs."
> From the voice of a devastated Earth a voice goes up
> with our own. It says: "Disarm! Disarm!
> The sword of murder is not the balance of justice."
> Let them meet first, as women, to bewail and
> commemorate the dead.
> Let them solemnly take counsel with each other as to
> the means
> whereby the great human family can live in peace...

Ann Jarvis, before she died in 1905, hoped for a national holiday to celebrate mothers. Her daughter Anna spent many years urging Congress and three presidents to support this idea, and in 1914 President Woodrow Wilson signed a bill for the national holiday. At first, the day was celebrated by attending church and writing letters to mothers. More and more, though, it was celebrated with presents, and flowers. Anna felt that the real meaning of honoring mothers became a way that businesses could promote and advertise their products so that they could sell them and make a profit. It was a way of saying that if you don't buy your Mother a gift, you don't appreciate her. This made Anna very sad and a little angry.

It is a good time to remember the caring qualities that most often are attributed to moms. *That doesn't mean that dads don't have those qualities.* Women have been great promoters of peace, and when they protest in a group, they don't seem to care what people think about them. They care too much for their children and families to worry about how someone else sees them.

However you celebrate your mothers, I am sure they will be pleased. Give them our love.

OXOXOX,

Grandma and Grandpa

30

Birthdays

May 14, 05

Dear Grand Children,

Yesterday Morgan was two years old. You all can count to two; you might even be able to count in Spanish, - uno, dos, - and in French, - un, deux. And you can easily write it in Roman numerals, I, II.

Today your Grandfather is seventy. Some of you may not be able to count that far, and if you can, you could try it in Spanish or French and I know some of you will be able to do that. If you write to seventy in Roman numerals, you will end with LXX.

Grandpa's birthday spankings would take a long time! You would get a sore arm and a stinging palm, and he would not want to sit down. Can you imagine a birthday cake with 70 candles? By the time they were all lit, the first ones would be burnt out. We could use ordinary candles, but they wouldn't fit on a cake, and probably not even the table! Your Grandpa is seventy!

When Grandpa was born, a loaf of bread was ten cents. Seventy years ago cars looked like black boxes with a smaller box in the front to hold the engine. His Grandfather Tony Mayer patented an idea for a trunk to be attached to the back which he made and sold. It was a black box that fit onto the bumper. Now our cars have trunks that are not attachments, and our cars are designed in all sorts of styles and colors.

Grandpa enjoys learning new things. He reads several books every week, and gets a lot of information on the computer. He enjoys gardening, studying and marveling at how plants grow. He observes the birds in our backyard, and discovered one which is part albino (white), with a white head and grey colored feathers. At times he becomes annoyed by the rabbits and squirrels which do harm to the garden.

He became a teacher and coach, thoroughly enjoying his students who still tell him that they appreciated his classes. He continues to teach with an email newsletter that combines his political, social and economic concerns with his values for the global family.

He loves you all very much. As you get older, you are appreciating his humor and teasing, and some of you tease him back now. He breathes you love and peace, and I ask you to breathe him love and peace today, too.

With love to our Hearts' Delights,

Grandma

31

Exclusion

May 15, 05

Dear Grand Children,

We belong to the global family! We need each other so that we all have enough food, sharing our work to make that happen. We need to live in a safe home, so we help to make our neighborhood safe for everyone. And we need each other for having some fun!

Sometimes neighbors disagree and then don't speak to each other, and children too can have friendships end, sometimes without knowing why. We may not get to know a person because he or she was born with a skin color different from ours, so the skin color becomes a barrier. Sometimes women are not treated fairly where they work, earning lower wages than the men. Sometimes we just don't act like a global family!

Your parents want you to be safe, and tell you which people would not be good friends and what places you should avoid. Pay attention to that and remember that Earth is sacred and we all are family. Breathe love and health to the people and places that your parents tell you are a danger.

When we were young, a black and white person marrying each other broke a governmental law but that discriminating law is now gone. At that time, too, in some communities African-American children could attend only a public school assigned to blacks and could drink only at water fountains for blacks; these laws also are gone. White children suffered, too, because those restrictions made it very difficult to make new friends with African-American children.

We are the losers when we lack understanding about our global family members, and then division and exclusion happen. Be inquisitive and ask questions about the things you don't understand. Why do the children at the end of the block attend a different school? Why do some women wear scarves on their heads? Why do we celebrate Kwanzaa?

A few friends of ours are gays and lesbians (people who feel an attraction to a person of the same sex; women are lesbians; men are gay). They would like the same privileges that married couples have; to be contacted in case of an accident and informed of their partner's condition. They would like to feel comfortable telling others about their special friendship, of their love and commitment to helping each other on their life journey. We don't live that lifestyle, but we understand their wanting those things for each other. We know several gay and lesbian couples; they are caring, nurturing, peaceful, and loving people. Sometimes they wear a rainbow sash at church to let others know that even though they are gay or lesbian, they are part of the global family. A Catholic bishop warned them to not come to receive communion wearing a sash this Sunday.

At St. Stephens' liturgy today we were invited to wear sashes to share the concerns of our gay and lesbian brothers and sisters. We chose to support our inclusive family. Dear ones, breathe healing, love and peace to those with different lifestyles, cultures, and religions. We are lured by the infinite variety and beauty of our Universe, and your breath connects you with that Creative Spirit of the Universe to mend this world.

Peace and love to our Healers,

Grandma and Grandpa

32

In Winnipeg

May 24, 05

Dear Grand Children,

We were in wonderful Winnipeg in May visiting Teresa and her family. A cultural meeting place for Lebanese is near their home. At the end of the block is a Spanish church. Ukrainians have a large community in Winnipeg, coming many years ago from the Ukraine, the "Breadbasket" of Russia. Other immigrants from all over the world have communities in this cosmopolitan city. Teresa is an immigrant! All grocery items are printed in English and French because Canada is bilingual.

More than one out of ten persons here are First Nation people, called Native Americans in the U.S. First Nation people who have married other nationalities are not counted in this 10 percent, so we see more on the streets who have Native features, dark skin color, dark straight hair, Native facial contours and body silhouette.

Many entrepreneurs (on trah prah NEWERS) have set up their own businesses. Just one block away from where Teresa and her family live is a woodworking store that sells all kinds of tools and teaches woodworking classes. A restaurant a few doors away teaches and sells its food creations as well as cooking utensils.

We watched Eamon play soccer and hockey while we were there. He is a talented boy, and his grandparents in Winnipeg help him get where he needs to be for his activities. Kaylee also enjoys sports, playing soccer and getting in some running when she has the time. Shea was in Minneapolis with his high school chorus, performing for two schools there; he returned to Winnipeg on Saturday.

Saturday evening we watched Connor in a ballet, the Secret Garden. From the movement of the dancers you would have seen anger, sadness, excitement, wonder, delight, confusion, fear, gratitude, joy. Some dancers showed us the wind, some became water and rain, some were fire. The costumes and stage lighting helped to interpret the wind, rain, and fire. We especially liked the fire costumes; on the darkened stage, rotating lights on the dancers made their sleeves layered with flame-like tongues seem real.

Ballet is an art form of dance, showing us the beauty and the ability to move our bodies in a great many ways. Music, ballet and sports are mystical-magical ways of creating beauty.

With much love,

Grandma and Grandpa

33

Jackson

May 25, 05

Dear Grand Children,

Congratulations! You were joined by Jackson Maniaci last evening as one of our grand children, the fourteenth. He weighed 6 lbs. 9 oz., and has lots of black hair. We heard him cry over the phone, a good sign that his lungs are developed and that he has a voice to eventually tell us his dreams and desires.

Each newborn is a miracle, formed from two cells combining and living within the protection of its mother's womb. The womb is the place beneath the mother's heart where a baby's fastest growth occurs for about nine months before it investigates the larger world. Truly a mystery, the body and soul develop together and are so integrated—blended—that one does not exist without the other in this life. Both come from the Creator who has designed each of us with our uniqueness.

How did this blending of body and spirit happen? How are family traits and features combined into this person? What new attributes and ambitions will he have and where will they come from? What new ideas will Jackson bring us? How can this happen with each new baby? These questions entice us to marvel at the Spirit of the Universe who provides infinite possibilities for each of us.

Thousands of years ago, women were recognized for their creative powers and the ability to provide food and a safe home in the womb before a baby was born. This was such a marvelous and spiritual experience that people worshipped goddesses. Today Christians, Jews, and Muslims have One God, but call their God by many names—Holy One, Provider, Shepherd, Gaia, Spirit, Wisdom, Yahweh, Creator,

Sophia, Shekinah, Allah—and there are others that you may have heard. Shekinah is a feminine word for "the presence of God." Sophia, a name meaning wisdom, and Gaia are two other feminine words for God.

We are grateful that Jackson is healthy, and for his parents who are co-creators with the Divinity. The Creator blesses our family and showers us with abundant gifts. We are thankful for the love of the Spirit which dwells within each of us and fills our world with enchantment.

Love to all our Delights,

Grandma and Grandpa

Jackson's Baptism

Jackson and his parents & sister Renata

Looking for fish

68

34

Jen's Birthday

May 26, 05

Dear Grand Children,

Your Aunt Jennifer is thirty-four years old today! She may be short in stature—some of you already are taller than she—but she is long on energy and talent. Have any of you tried to play basketball or softball with her? This summer may be a good time to challenge her, because she is carrying your next cousin under her heart, and that will slow her down a little bit.

She likes to play games and is truly competitive, so when you need another person for a card game or for golf, she is the person to ask. That may be a problem for you, though, unless you live in Denver.

As an organizer, Jen ranks with the best. She began a fun run in Grand Forks, North Dakota when she and Lee lived there. It continued after she moved because the runners had fun and she left good plans to follow. Most of us were in Denver to enjoy a great 2003 Christmas vacation, skiing and snow boarding, visiting the Red Rock arena, attending a University of Denver hockey game, and playing games late into the night. Besides that, we had enough food for everyone to enjoy, which takes planning and preparation.

Have you ever had fun breaking a piñata at our family gatherings? The piñata was a Mayer tradition that began with Easter on the Waterloo farm, but they were bought at a store and easier to break than those that Jen has created.

Whenever you need to be cheered up, she is able to direct your thoughts to uplifting memories about yourself. To know this about her is to know one way of helping yourself when you are feeling out-of-sorts and a bit sad or anxious, because she knows about disappointments, failure, and sacrifice. When she failed a class, she relentlessly worked for an A. She and Lee endured living in different places in the U.S. so that she could become a Physician's Assistant, a sacrifice for both of them. Her greatest help to you might be her example of *finding enjoyment in the common, everyday events,* - a walk in the park, a run or bike ride, planting and tending a garden, singing with Morgan, petting Moose (the dog), doing "rounds" visiting her patients in the hospital, preparing food and eating it, vacuuming with Morgan, playing the piano.

Celebrate with her today by breathing your good wishes to her. Our lives are bound with hers, and the love and peace we send to her with every breath will spread like a flood to everyone.

Our love and peace,

Grandma and Grandpa

35

On the Farm

June 7, 05

Dear Grand Children,

We had an adventure in Winnipeg. We drove to a farm that Chris owns where he built his home, and you would have enjoyed using the ladder to get to the sleeping loft.

There is no water faucet in the house, so we brought drinking water. For washing dishes or cleaning up, he dips water from a stream nearby. Our towns have polluted our rivers and streams with fertilizers and trash, and the bubbles we sometimes see in our waterways come from oil or liquid chemicals that someone dumped into it. Chris does not use chemicals on his gardens. The water on the farm is pristine (prisTEEN)—fresh and clean.

The gardens will produce strawberries, corn, tomatoes and other vegetables. They are in small plots around the house and enclosed with tall fencing to keep out deer and other animals. Chris planted some of his garden, and Teresa weeded the strawberry patch while we were there.

A stove in the house heats the one big room and the loft above it. Chris chops wood from his farm, and stacks it to use when it is cold. Jack Pine and Tamarack trees are found in the wooded areas. Tamarack is denser and burns slower, so it is a better wood for burning.

Bear live in the area, feeding on berries. Once they find other sources of food, especially at a farm, they return for more. They can be annoying and a nuisance. Maybe that's why the pioneers had bear rugs! We didn't see any bear while we were there.

Eamon likes playing at the farm. Connor wanted to take us on a hike, but with so much rain before we came, the ground was soaked, making it a marshland. Shea also spent time at the farm, singing songs from his trip to Minneapolis and even singing the soprano part! He also played the guitar and sang LOUD. Kaylee worked the day we were there.

Electricity for the home is generated by the sun. Chris has installed solar panels. In the summer, there is more daylight on the farm than any of you have who live in the United States. When they want to use the radio, they wait for a sunny day so that they don't deplete their electricity.

Some of us would not like to live without being able to turn on a faucet, to turn up the thermostat, or to switch on the TV or DVD. Teresa and her family find it refreshing and relaxing. They drop their worries for awhile and absorb the beauty and fresh air at the farm.

Love to you and your parents,

Grandma and Grandpa

36

Stereotypes

June 8, 05

Dear Grand Children,

What is a stereotype? Stereo means something solid, three-dimensional. *Stereotype* was first used to mean a metal printing plate, and *stereotypers* printed the same thing over and over. Stereotype came to mean a routine or same old mental picture over and over about customs, people, places.

Stereotypes! Blonds are dumb. Black is a sign of darkness, fear, evil. Teenage drivers are speedy. Redheads are hot-headed, quick to get angry. Terrible twos. Sunny California.

These stereotypes are not always true. Teenagers are just learning to drive, but they don't cause all of the accidents. We have some blond grand children, but none of them are dumb. Two-year olds find out they have an opinion and want to tell everyone what it is, but it isn't always terrible. About redheads, surely that stereotype doesn't always fit the person! (Smile here for our red-headed family members.)

A few more stereotypes: Librarians are prim, proper, and "stuffy." Husbands "rule the roost." Long haired people are unconventional and like classical music. Old age is all down-hill. These examples really don't fit Grandma, who is 70 years old today. She was a librarian, but she never considered herself "stuffy." Husband Joe doesn't always rule the roost; both of them do cackle at each other. Long haired people—hmmm, that might fit although her hair sometimes is short. "Old age is all down-hill" is a joke because it all depends on whether the person keeps busy with reading, gardening, doing house beautification (chores), making music, challenging all those stereotypes.

Challenging stereotypes can be fun. Grandma still questions cultural, religious, political, and environmental doctrines (rules), even more than before.

She likes some of the Native American ways that confront stereotypes. They honor their elders (people who are older--and wiser?) by asking them for advice. They honor those they love by giving them time and attention. They honor their young by allowing them to become who they are intended to be. They honor each other by listening without interrupting. Sometimes they honor by gentle joking. They are generous with their possessions, giving them away because someone needs it more or loves it more. They honor others with song and dance at their gatherings. It all amounts to respect for others, for their possessions, and for the universe.

Today if Grandma were Native American, she would be giving you presents! Bless her with your breath, and she breathes you her blessings.

Love to our Unique Breathers,

Grandma and Grandpa

37

Garden Magic

June 9, 05

Dear Grand Children,

This morning working in the garden, we observed again how the Maple Tree regenerates. You all have seen the helicopters—the seeds that form on Maples early in the spring—fall and spin to the ground. Off the tree, they seem to be dead, but we haven't been able to actually see what happens after that.

The next thing we know, a clump of many helicopters, flat end to the ground, have been absorbed into the soil. How it happens is a mystery to us. How do they come together and how do their flat ends become buried? How do the light ends become buried and the heavy ends protrude from the ground? How do they know that coming together for this dance into the soil gives a better chance for survival? The propeller part obviously contains the root; it finds nourishment as it burrows lower for its developing roots, and the bulb end turns green as it ripens and unfurls, becoming two leaves.

Maples have regeneration planned into their molecules and atoms. They are prolific (very productive, fertile), and seem to make sure that they continue to live. It is a benefit to us, but we also don't want a yard full of Maples, so we uproot those little shoots, and tend to the trees that we already have.

Another miracle is the way fir trees reproduce. We have many small pine cones in one garden patch, and we find some frail tiny fir sprouts. We can appreciate how long it takes for them to become a viable (able to thrive) plant. In a forest they may become trampled, but their survival is better there than in our gardens and grass. Squirrels dig and rabbits eat lots of young green things, plus a lawnmower and a hoe threaten their wild production.

We appreciate our garden miracles. We look at our plants every day, but can't actually see the new leaf or blossom develop. Yet it happens. They bless us with variety, food, beauty, delight, aroma, color, magic, wonder.

And you know what? You, too, bless us with variety, food (for thought), beauty, delight, aroma (well, maybe not always good aroma), color, magic and wonder!

Much love to our Magical Wonders,

Grandma and Grandpa

38

Great Uncle Mike

June 18, 05

Dear Grand Children,

On Wednesday, your Great-Uncle Mike Mraz from Atlanta flew to Minnesota to attend a court hearing about his son's death. His son, Jonathan, was killed by a train in October 2003 as he was walking home on railroad tracks. He had been at a party where he drank some beer and liquor, and had been drinking before he arrived there. When a person drinks too much or has taken drugs, he or she then becomes irrational (not sensible or reasonable).

By the time Jon left the party, he was not able to think reasonably, or at least his mind and reflexes were slower. People drink for many reasons; to mask a problem or because others are doing it, because it is forbidden, to prove you can drink a lot, or a number of other reasons. Drinking can become an addiction (a habit that is difficult to overcome). The only solution to alcohol addiction, which is a medical problem, is to not drink any liquor at all.

The woman who allowed the party at her house was in court because she supplied liquor and beer to minors (people who are not yet old enough to use alcohol) at her home. She admitted her mistake, and will be sentenced to probation or time in prison for not getting help for Jon, and for allowing underage drinking in her home. Probation is a weekly appointment with an official of the court to report how she spent the week. She needs to follow the law—no more parties for underage persons.

Life is precious, with many possible adventures and wondrous experiences, and we wish that for all of you. You know how to take care of yourselves, to eat healthy foods, to exercise to keep a healthy body, and to avoid dangerous situations. You also need to maintain a healthy spirit, so go to your parents or someone you respect when you need to talk about a problem or when you experience a big disappointment or when something puzzles you.

Mike greatly misses his son, prays for him and to him, weeps for him, wishes that his life could have been longer, and wants everyone who had a part in supplying or encouraging Jon's drinking to realize their deadly mistake. Mike doesn't want this tragedy to happen to any other children. Yet nothing can bring Jon back. He is safe now and in a better place, even though we can't see him. We can breathe peace and love for all the people who were part of Jon's life, so that they find serenity, and that they appreciate the joy and delight that Jon brought to them while he was still with them. Especially breathe peace and love to your Great-Uncle Mike, so that his sadness heals and he can bless Jonathan's new life. We know you will want to do this for him.

Love to our Breathing Beauties,

Grandma and Grandpa

39

Father's Day

June 19, 05

Dear Grand Children,

It takes a long time for some dreams to become real. In 1909, almost one hundred years ago, a woman wanted to honor her Dad with a special day. The first Father's Day was celebrated in 1910 in a town in Washington State. In 1924, President Calvin Coolidge liked the idea of a day to celebrate fathers. Then President Lyndon Johnson signed a proclamation for Father's Day on the third Sunday in June in 1966, but the day wasn't set aside every year until President Nixon in 1972 made it a permanent holiday. It took 63 years from start to finish for that idea to become real. When we were growing up, Father's Day was not always celebrated.

Tomorrow is Father's Day, and I'm wondering how many of you will buy or make your Dad a tie? That is the favorite gift for fathers. Silk, cotton, wool, leather, string, rope, linen, lace, and synthetic materials have been used to make ties.

If there is a vain vein (both words sound the same but have different meanings: vain means proud, and vein means a line or thread running through the body.) Let's begin again. If there is a vain vein in your father, (a proud streak running through him) you could glimpse it in the style of his tie. You may have seen old pictures of men proudly wearing lace cravats around their necks, and the men probably wore a powdered wig, too. That style today would not make your father feel vain.

A hundred years ago, a prize fighter from England began wearing a blue silk scarf with polka dots around his neck. Now who is going to laugh at a prize fighter if he wears something silly? Cowboys in western U.S. wore this practical style because on windy days, they could pull it over their noses to keep out the dust. These bandannas were colorful,—green, brown, black, and sometimes pink and yellow. They were printed with flowers or bird's eyes or other patterns, or tie-dyed.

Colonel Sanders who created Kentucky-fried chicken, wore a plantation tie that is a ribbon tied into a bow. He is always pictured with his tie, popular on U.S. plantations when our nation was still young. One man wove leather together and attached bells to the ends and ran it through a turquoise buckle; it was called a bolo because it resembled rope that Argentine cowboys used to capture cattle. The bolo is the official necktie in Arizona.

Ties were created from hatbands; some were decorated with brooches or pins. If you choose to make a tie, whether you make a bandanna, plantation tie from ribbon, bolo from leather string, bowtie, cravat from lace, or design your own tie, your Dad will be pleased. But don't be disappointed if he doesn't wear it to work and chooses instead to save it as a special remembrance of the day.

Dads are special. They feel a great responsibility to make your lives easier than their own. They want to protect you from danger and pain. They manage to stay strong when they would rather cry. They are your greatest cheerleaders—well, your moms are, too—because they love you. Give them a hug for us.

We love you,

Grandma and Grandpa

40

Wasting Food

June 24, 05

Dear Grand Children,

Twice this week we read about the amount of food that is wasted in the United States. Can you guess how much we waste?

Our garden is producing lettuce and Swiss chard, and we will have some to give away. Our peas are forming, and over the years we have shared them with our winged relatives. Birds like our raspberries, too, so Grandpa picks them early in the morning before the birds have them for breakfast, but then sometimes Grandpa is breakfast for the mosquitoes!

We are trying eggplant this year. It is a beautiful deep purple shade and grows in the shape of a huge egg; some are bigger than your hand. We have a few recipes we want to try with it, and if you come late in the summer or early fall, you can have a taste. We hope it tastes as good as it looks!

Our neighbors decided to plant a garden this year, and we think it is because we asked them to harvest our produce last year when we were gone. They picked tomatoes, and fried the green ones that they sliced and dipped in a batter. It was a mouth-watering treat to them but we don't appreciate fried green tomatoes as much as our neighbors. The adventure of a new taste is better if we choose just a tiny bit to sample at first.

When we cook, we have left-overs, very nice to reheat for another meal or to freeze for a later time. When we buy a watermelon, we will invite you because we can't finish one by ourselves. It gets mushy when it is frozen, so it can't be stored.

Plants are miraculous in the ways they grow and supply food for us. Each plant has a unique taste. That food becomes part of us, and we are transformed (changed) by it. It is a mystery how everything in nature all works together. And our Creator's design of nature is spellbinding. What better time to think about that than at the dinner table? What better place to encounter the Spirit of the Universe than in the food that blesses us with tastes, aromas, textures, colors, and shapes?

Even though we have an abundance of food, we should not waste it. If you guessed that half of our food in the United States is wasted, you would be correct. That includes the loss that happens harvesting and processing it.

Love to our culinary adventurers,

Grandma and Grandpa

41

Larva

June 26, 05

Dear Grand Children,

Out in our lawn we spied something moving. At a distance we could tell it was a fuzzy kind of caterpillar, climbing the blades of grass and zigzagging toward our big tree. With a closer view, we discovered that it looked fuzzy because it had whiskers all over its upper body.

Our Insect Guide Book identified it as the baby of a White-Marked Tussock Moth, and what we saw was really called a larva. It had a small red head and two tufts of black whiskers that were like antenna, and another tuft of brown that looked like a tail. All the other whiskers were white, and it was beautiful, much better than the picture in our book.

Down its back was a thin black stripe. Behind its head and along the stripe were whiskers extending halfway down its back which looked like a solid line until it moved, and then we could tell it was four thick tufts. Further down the back and in the stripe were two tiny red triangles. As the larva moved, we could see the yellowish green underbelly and its pair of six stubby legs. It used its mouth and legs to climb the grass. It would bend and fall because of its weight on the thin grass, or bend that blade and twist forward.

The larva seemed to prefer climbing the grass, inefficiently moving up and down rather than across. It seemed to have a destination; it was constantly moving. We watched it for more than a half-hour but we had other things to do, so we don't know what became of it.

These larvae are found in most parts of the United States, but not along the West Coast. They can be a pest because they like ornamental trees for food. Maybe the larva we saw was in a hurry because it didn't want to become dinner for the birds that come to feast in our yard!

Insects are important to our world. Without them we would have no apples, grapes, clover, or other plants because some of them pollinate the flowers. Some insects help the process of decay. Some control other insects. All of them together help to keep the balance of nature.

The first people who lived on Mother Earth believed that Earth was One Living Being composed of many parts, and that we are one of the parts along with our winged and animal cousins, and, yes, even those insects. Everything on Earth comes from our Creator who delights in this diversity of life and we are grateful for its wonderful display.

Love to our Delightful Wonders,

Grandma and Grandpa

42

Not Random or Determined

July 15, 05

Dear Grand Children,

Looking at the calendar, we discovered that, oh no, next year on this date Joseph Donald will become a Teenager! He is growing up too fast, and too soon he will be asking for the car keys!

Jackson and Luke are growing faster than any of you. If you are growing at their rate, people might think you have an eating disorder. Your youngest cousins will have added one-third more to their weight by the time they are two months old. If you weigh 80 pounds now, adding one-third to your weight would put you over 106 pounds.

Each person gains weight according to the amount they eat, their metabolism (how their body processes and changes food into energy), and how active they are. You each have different rates of metabolism, different choice of foods, and different activities, so you each are unique. This is not random (having no definite pattern) and it is not determined (having a precise pattern); it is creative, having several possibilities.

Let us explain it another way. This afternoon we listened to some beautiful music that was taped at the Red Rocks amphitheater in Denver. Some of the music was improvised, which means it was not written and probably won't ever be played in the same way again. It was not random because it fit the tempo and melody, but it was not determined because it was not the written music. It was creative because the musician was "ad libbing" the music by varying the rhythm or the melody to make it different, interesting, whimsical and /or funny.

Nature is not random or determined. It is creative. Our animal and flying relatives experience the same creative patterns. None of them eat exactly the same things or have the same growth rates, so they are unique also. We are blessed with this wondrous gift of diversity in nature; it expands our encounters with the Spirit of the Universe and stretches our imaginations.

The Divine is unfolding in Creation, and we can see, smell, touch, hear, and taste the Spirit in this emerging world. Everything is holy because it all comes from the Spirit. Our world is not perfect, though; we humans do not always understand or act in ways that benefit Earth. Join us; breathe peace and love to the Universe, and you will help bring healing and forgiveness to the world and to our global family.

Love to our Creative Healers,

Grandma and Grandpa

43

Jackson's Baptism

Aug 18, 05

Dear Grand Children,

Are you wondering about Jackson's baptism and whether he got dunked in the lake? He didn't wear a wetsuit because he didn't get to plunge underwater, but we suspect that he would have communicated his feelings about that! He sang us a solo once during his celebration!

We thanked the Spirit of the Universe for Jackson and welcomed him into the world where our Creator designed the four-legged animals and the winged creatures, who set the stars in the firmament and who breathed life into our first parents, and called ALL of it "good."

We celebrated Mike and Becky's commitment to provide Jackson's needs, to support him with direction, and to encourage him as he explores his inner and outer universe. We thanked his Godparents for their willingness to find opportunities for Jackson's spiritual growth.

We welcomed Jackson into the Christian community where Jesus teaches us to live as his brothers and sisters in the huge and inclusive family of God. Do you remember that Jesus beckoned the children to come to him? He charmed them with stories, played with them and we suspect he taught them how to fish. Well, we also have a responsibility to Jackson. We are to bring Jesus, to be Jesus, to Jackson in our story-telling and companionship to him.

Grandpa and Grandma were asked to offer a prayer. It was appropriate to pray at the Lake, a part of God's holy and beautiful Creation. We thanked God for Jackson who is holy because he too comes from God. He—and we—can never be separated from the Divine Spirit who loves us without end.

Jackson enjoyed having water scooped from the lake and poured over his forehead by Dennis who conducted the Baptism, and his parents and Godparents scooped some more on him. Then Dennis, who is a cousin to Jackson's Dad, lifted him up high so he could see the world and the world could see him. We clapped and some of us even brushed away a tear because of the inspiring ceremony.

Your Great Aunt Leanna and some of her family attended the Baptism; she likes to call herself Leanna the Great. Remember that when you see her again. Your Aunts Mary Beth and Ann, and cousins John, Ellie, Patty, Caroline and Tim were there to help celebrate. Jackson's Grandma Rose, Mike's mother who is 85 years old, also came to honor Jackson. We wish you could have been there, too.

With love,

Grandma and Grandpa

44

Seventieth Birthday

Aug 24, 05

Dear Grand Children,

So OK, you proved you really can keep a secret! The porta-potty was the first clue that something was up last weekend at the lake, and Aunt Becky's weird smile when she came to welcome us was the second one. And in the car on the way there, if we had tuned in to what Teresa and her sons were doing in the backseat, we might have been able to figure out why she kept asking how much time we had before we got to the cottage. She had her phone on to let the surprisers know how soon we would be there! Very clever!

We thought the celebration of our seventieth birthdays was over. Grandpa was so shocked that he forgot to growl at you to "Don't have fun!" Grandma would have worried for days and nights about feeding so many people, but your parents had all of it worked out with teams for each meal. We were stuck with "having fun" because there was nothing else for us to do!

The lake looked perky with all of the colorful floats and games. It may have caused a lot of pontoon traffic at our end by curious people wondering about all the commotion. They probably were happy that they didn't have to feed and provide a sleep-over for that many people. They must have been impressed with the many games and activities they saw for you; it was great planning on the part of your parents.

Becky and Mike are generous with their cottage, an opportunity for all of us to relax and enjoy its serenity. We share it with the wild creatures that venture out when they think it is safe. Coyotes were singing on Saturday night. Sometimes you can hear the bullfrogs burp and mourning doves whoodle. If you are lucky, you might spy a Sandhill Crane meandering along the shore searching for food.

You like picking up snails and fishing off the dock. Turtles and ducks paddle by, close enough to satisfy their curiosity but far enough away that we don't scare them. Loons, Minnesota's state bird that does not know enough to stay in its own state, go fishing in the lake. Loons have a mournful and strange call, usually heard at night during migration. Their eyes can focus in and out of the water, and they pump oxygen into their legs so that they can dive 200 feet for their dinner. A football field is 300 feet, so they can go very deep.

The only disappointment for the surprise birthday celebration was that 140 candles were not on the cake. Or would that have brought the Rural Fire Department to investigate all the smoke and flames? You don't have to surprise us with a birthday party again until next year!

We cherish our Grand Children,

Grandma and Grandpa

Seventieth Surprise Birthday Party

Front: Joe, Teresa, Ben
Back: Sarah, Jen, Becky, Andy, Mary

45

Odds and Ends

Aug 31, 05

Dear Grand Children,

Connor arrived at our house last evening from San Francisco with his Dad, Glen, and Glen's friend Teresa. Glen is beginning a new job in Rhode Island, and his friend will visit her family who lives in that area, and then she will fly back to San Francisco on Friday to attend a wedding.

Today, Connor used some work-out equipment at a fitness store where we were looking at bikes. He slept late this morning, but tomorrow we are getting up early to drive him back to Winnipeg, a good start for training himself to get up for school. He brought back some new running shoes and some spiked shoes for cross-country. He will be a busy fellow this school year!

This afternoon, Grandma bought a bike, and it has a basket on it so she can go shopping. It was ready to pick up this evening, so she rode it home and ended up with rubber legs. It will take her some time to get in shape.

Our garden is prolific! We are giving away lots of eggplant and pickles. Grandma made some dill pickles for your Uncle Joe for his visit in September, but he came early for our surprise birthday party, so he didn't get to eat them. Does anyone else like dill pickles? You will have to try our green tomato jam. It tastes very good. And we also have elderberry jelly made from the berries that hung over the fence from our neighbor's yard. It turned out delicious.

Grandpa has been going through the clinic again because he has balance problems and lacks energy. To try to feel better, he decided to drop wheat from his diet. He is not eating any ordinary bread, and gave up eating cake and cookies. We bought some rice bread which tastes good, and Grandma made some cornbread last evening, but it doesn't hold together and wouldn't make a good sandwich. We will try a recipe for a flat round bread like a taco made with millet flour. When you visit again you can try all these new foods! We are having an adventure with these new tastes, and sometimes the adventure is good, and sometimes it's....interesting!

Love,

Grandma and Grandpa

46

Motorcycle

Sept 11, 05

Dear Grand Children,

This noon while we were eating, we wondered what it would be like to have a motorcycle with a side-car. Can you imagine the fun we could have with a toy like that? Then we thought it would be better to have a motorcycle with a trailer.

A motorcycle would be an easy way to get in and out of traffic, it would get good gas mileage, and would be a hoot to ride. On the other hand, it would not be practical in the rain, in winter, or on windy days. Our balance will have to be good, and we would have to pack carefully.

What would you do if we drove up to your house in a motorcycle? Would your parents let you go on a ride with us? Can you picture us in black leather jackets with a scarf around our necks, and big helmets on our heads? Should we get leather pants and boots to go with the jackets?

Motorcyclists need to look mod, so we would have to expand our wardrobes. We would want to take lessons in driving one to feel safe. Grandpa would have to let his hair grow. We would want to learn about the mechanics of it so that we would know what to do if it decided to stop working.

Two of your uncles—that we know of—own or have owned motorcycles, and your Great Uncle Chuck, husband of Leanna the Great, also rode one with the intention of buying it. Chuck, who died a few years ago, felt lucky to have survived that ride to tell about it. He never had the desire to ride another motorcycle again, unusual for a man who seemed fearless.

Parents, especially mothers, are likely to worry when their children buy one. Your Great Aunt Carolyn who was at our birthday party last month, was surprised when her son Tony, during his high school years, brought one home. She must have scolded him loud enough for the neighbors four blocks away to hear. They live next to a cemetery, and we think she disturbed the peace of those buried there. Tony never did get to ride it.

This motorcycle of ours is a dream and we are 99% sure that it will never be more than that, so I don't think you will see us riding a hog to your house any time soon. But it is fun to dream!

We breathe you peace, love, and health,

Grandma and Grandpa

47

Nine-eleven

Sept 11, 05

Dear Grand Children,

Today is your Uncle Mike Maniaci's birthday. His greatest present this year is the birth of Jackson. He knows how to quiet him, and loves making him smile. Michael would be living on the golf course if he hadn't met Becky; we are grateful that they met each other and that Mike is part of our family now.

Today also marks the fourth anniversary of the 9/11 terrorist attacks on New York, the Pentagon, and a plane that was diverted from another destination, some say from flying into the Whitehouse. It was a tragedy that so many innocent people died that day, and for something that they couldn't control. Terrorists are angry, desperate, and frustrated people willing to die for their cause. They have lost hope that things will get better for them any other way. One reason for their attack was that they wanted to drive out the United States army bases from Saudi Arabia. No nation has armed forces that can stand up to ours, so they resorted to terrorism.

You need to remember that their reasons for this attack were against our government and not our people. They hope that something better will come from dying for their cause. As more and more people find terrorism the only solution to the problems of the world, the world—that means you and we—needs to listen and respond with care for these members of our human family. It will be far from easy and for some it will be dangerous.

As you grow older, it is important for you to know the people who are elected to represent you in our government so you can share your opinions. You also will learn about the issues,—how our government responds to those who are poor and vulnerable members of our country's family and the global family. That is a huge responsibility, and you may not find it interesting. Yet some of you will want to participate in government to make this a better world. Your grandpa was a member of the Rochester City Council many years ago, and it took much time and study to be prepared for their meetings. It was a good experience for him and he helped our city make some good decisions.

Always you can breathe peace, healing and love to our global family. You do make a difference when you pray this way. While you are at it, breathe peace, love, and birthday blessings to your Uncle Michael.

We love our Awesome Wonders,

Grandma and Grandpa

48

Becky's Birthday

Sept 15, 05

Dear Grand Children,

Forty-two years ago, this date landed on a Sunday. Your Aunt Becky was born that afternoon, and she must have known even then that anyone born on a Sunday is "full of grace."

A delightful child, Becky never sat still long enough to have her hair trimmed, but her hair always needed more than trimming because it had a mind of its own. People didn't usually notice it, however, because she didn't stay in one place very long so that you could see it, and she liked to wear hats. Sometimes she wore hats and not much else!

Becky always brought friends to the house, and had a couple of boyfriends who walked with her to school when they were in kindergarten together. Once she and one of her neighborhood friends were in the back yard and we noticed smoke coming out of the lilac bushes. You might guess what they were doing; Grandpa had a talk with them, and her friend went home in a hurry.

Becky loves her nieces and nephews, and takes time to visit with all of you. She is generous with everything she has which has a way of multiplying your own things.

When you are ready to find work, I hope that you will find an employer who is as thoughtful as Becky. She has fun with the people she hires, pays them well and gives bonuses at the end of the year, gives them health and financial benefits, sometimes gives them an afternoon off when work is slow, and invites them on vacation weekends or to their lake home. Does that sound like a deal or what?

Creative, intelligent, loving, inquisitive, energetic, willing to take risks, fun-loving, generous, doing things for others when there is nothing to gain personally,—these are marks of grace. Do you notice that these marks really are gifts, because these are impossible to develop unless you have them? Becky is grace-filled and uses these gifts, and we are better off because of her.

But you are grace-filled, too. You all have these gifts, and all you have to do is take them up and use them. The Spirit of the Universe is the Source of them as well as of you. When you breathe in and out, you connect with that Source. Breathe these gifts for you and your families, and send a birthday blessing to your Aunt Becky.

Love to our Grace-filled Delights,

Grandma and Grandpa

49

Flickers

Sept 23, 05

Dear Grand Children,

Yesterday your cousin Kelli had her fourteenth birthday, and we know that she requested Frog Eye Salad. If she had celebrated her birthday in Rochester, she would have been able to have eggplant parmagiana and a choice of pickles for her menu, something zesty for the feast!

We have had some winged visitors the past week. Yellow-shafted Flickers are a bit longer than a Blue Jay, and have long beaks like a woodpecker. In fact, they are related to the woodpecker family, but these birds like to peck away in the ground as well as on trees. They have a grey head with a red stripe around the back of the head, like they are wearing a baseball cap turned around. They sport a black V necktie. Their breast is golden with black spots, wings gold to salmon colored. The males have a black mustache on either side of their bills. They wear a white band on their tails, and are more beautiful than their pictures. We have not seen them before even though they make their home year-round in Minnesota as well as south and east of here.

Our Flickers are shy of people, and when we go outside they scatter into the trees. They are a small flock, and it is easy to tell the youngsters because they have gone into our gardens with the low chicken-wire fence and then can't figure out how to get out. The parents don't seem concerned, though; they keep pecking away at the insects they find in the grass, and eventually they are joined by the young ones when they discover they can fly over the fence.

How do birds learn to fly? Do they need their parents to teach them? Have you seen some young birds hop after their parents and beg them to feed them? Sometimes the parents act as if they can't be bothered with them any more, and it could be that they are trying to teach their young ones by example how to find their own meals. How do they learn to distrust us and fly away when we come out of the house? Do birds remember? Do they have a brain? How did the first birds learn how to survive? We have too many questions!

We are amazed at the skills of our feathered relatives, and with their beauty and color. They dropped from the sky to entertain us for a week, but we haven't seen them now for two days. They probably stopped here for a meal and liked the menu that our yard offered them.

We breathe you our love and peace and send Kelli fourteen times fourteen birthday blessings. Breathe your love and birthday blessings to her, too.

Love you fourteen times fourteen,

Grandma and Grandpa

50

Andy's Birthday

Sept 30, 05

Dear Grand Children,

Today Andrew Timothy John-John Gugenheimer Winnie-the-Pooh Delicious-Guy Mayer is celebrating a birthday. We don't remember how he got so many names, and he may not remember, either. He was young when he received the delicious-guy name. He described something he was eating as delicious and we know it wasn't eggplant.

Andrew used to bring "crawdads" home from the creek in a bucket, curious about them. He and a neighbor liked to construct unusual go-carts that would almost roll, and other creations that had never been fashioned and haven't been repeated since.

You can't imagine the Haunted-House he created in the basement room of our old home that once was the "coal bin." His haunted-House had lots of flying things and dark curtains hanging from the ceiling; it was a parent's delight and dismay all at the same time!

He never wasted time when he was in high school. On a school morning, he was the last one to get up, sometimes getting into the shower after everyone else had gone to school, and arriving inside the classroom as the bell rang! Everyone was amazed at his ability to calculate how much time he could cut from his school day!

A guy of many talents with more to discover, he handles responsibility with one hundred percent concentration in anything he does—at work, at home, at school. Yup, he is going to school again, this time for a Master's degree, and enjoying the classes even though they are exhausting physically and mentally.

He learned a lesson in the oil fields in Colorado and Wyoming. He and his drilling crew would be at a site and sometimes were sent to another location without taking a break. It took a toll on his health, and he ended up aggravating a heart condition and needing a pacemaker. The lesson is that *you need to take care of yourself,*—get enough rest, eat healthy foods, and minimize stress.

Efficient, hard-working, having fun and creating fun, curious and talented, caring and forgiving, learning and sharing, Andy is celebrating FORTY years, and we hope Winnie-the-Pooh guy will be with you another forty years. Breathe blessings, love and peace to him.

Love to our Delicious Grand Children,

Grandma and Grandpa

Andy & Ann

Caroline, Tim & Patty

Grandpa reading to grandchildren

51

Colorado Trip and Luke's Birthday

Oct 1, 05

Dear Grand Children,

While our computer was having tantrums in July, we realized that our letter to you about our visit to Colorado was never sent, and the computer went to computer heaven and took our letter with it. So this is old news, but good news!

Morgan babysat us the first day of our visit on June 28, letting us know what food she liked and where to find it. She pulled out her toys and games and put them away when she finished although sometimes she needed to be reminded. A little more than twenty-five months old, she talked in sentences so that we could understand and help her. She loves books and thinks she knows how to read. She entertained us with songs, combining several together, and dances to every kind of music.

The next day, June 29th, Luke was born. She was prepared well by her parents for this new miracle, but we're sure that she didn't realize how it would turn life upside down for all of them. She truly loves him and learned that a gentle touch was not the same one she uses when she plays with dolls. We visited Luke in the hospital on his birth day when Mom Jennifer was not far on the road to recovery, fighting nausea. Jen had some irregular heart beats which concerned her doctor, so the baby was born with the help of surgery.

For two more days we visited Luke, and each day Morgan really wanted to stay, but came home with us without a fuss. Dad Lee also stayed at the hospital two nights, a very good innovation since your parents were born. Aunt Sarah was a great help in making Morgan feel comfortable.

Saturday everyone came home from the hospital and we all went to an evening concert in the park. We're sure that Luke was the youngest one there. A day or two later, Jen, Morgan, Luke and Grandma walked to the neighborhood park. It was HOT that day, yet Jen and Morgan enjoyed the sunny playground while Luke and Grandma wilted in the shade.

Luke probably was five days old when your Aunt Jen ran circles around Grandma while they were hauling tree trimmings to the street for the garbage collectors. We realized then it was time to go home; Jen's energy was restored!

Luke is a gift to us all, a miracle of life, a blessing of Creation. You, too, are miracles, and so is the global family, our animal cousins and Earth home. We breathe our gratitude to the Spirit of the Universe.

Love to our Miracles,

Grandma and Grandpa

52

Aunt Agnes

Oct 9, 05

Dear Grand Children,

We received word that my Aunt Agnes Muehe, my mother's youngest sister, died in her sleep on September 16th. She would be your great-great aunt. She was eighty-eight years old, lived in Oregon, and survived some medical problems, living longer than her doctor had predicted.

She was the first one to send me a grown-up valentine. Her striking salt-and-pepper hair and smile wrinkles on the outer edges of her eyes were something I thought I would like when I was older. Her eyes sparkled with humor, and she had a dignified but relaxed manner.

Visiting with her in February, 2002, she told us she had been a tomboy when she grew up because most of her playmates were boys when they lived on a farm near Bancroft, Iowa. She remembered coming home from country school with Mildred (my mother) during a snowstorm, carrying their lunch pail, and seeing their mother watching for them from the top of a hill.

We sat on her deck in shirtsleeves that day, admiring the lush, green mountain, an old and cherished friend to her. She considered Oregon to be the most beautiful place she had ever lived.

Her husband, John, had a stroke in 1972 which left him partially paralyzed and mentally impaired, but he moved around with a cane and enjoyed watching TV programs. A big man, he became unsteady on his feet and when he fell, Aunt Agnes would call the fire department for help. When his falls were too frequent, he moved to a nursing home, living there not quite a year before he died peacefully in 1992.

Aunt Agnes worked for many years after Uncle John had his stroke, and we know she was appreciated by her co-workers for her work ethic and cheerful attitude. And when they wanted to know how to spell a word, they always asked her!

Aunt Agnes did not want a funeral Mass because she didn't like funerals. She requested to be cremated and her ashes scattered in the ocean. She loved an outdoor grotto near her home and since her death, many Masses have been offered for her there. This relative comes from generations of good people who are part of your ancestral family. Think of her when you need a positive thought for your day.

I breathe you peace and love,

Grandma

53

Good News and Other News

Oct 15, 05

Dear Grand Children,

This morning there was an accident next door. A young man was helping his neighbor work on his car. He thought the car was in proper gear, but while he was under it, the car started to roll backward and he was bent into a kneeling position. The steering wheel was turned so that it stopped at our front lawn. Some of the neighbors heard his cry for help and lifted off the car so that he could crawl out. While we were waiting for the ambulance, we got him some pillows and blankets to make him comfortable.

By the time the ambulance arrived, two police cars and one of the fire rescue trucks was on our street in response to the accident. By that time, he was shivering, probably because he was in shock. The injured man had lit up a cigarette after he was freed, and one of the fire rescue team members ordered him to put it out because it would add stress to his heart.

The man doesn't have any broken bones and was dismissed from the hospital five hours after he arrived. He has some torn ligaments which can be more painful than a fracture and will take months to heal, and some skin burns from being dragged by the car.

This week Grandma started exercising her bike every day for two days. She intended to do it every day, but it didn't last long. We hope you are more successful with your intentions.

She also tried a new flat bread recipe that should have made a soft taco. The flour she used was millet, not common here in the U.S., and after she tasted it, she knew that Grandpa would not like it and she wasn't sure that the birds would like it, either. The recipe that came from Africa was thrown out after the first taste. If the birds don't eat it, the good news is that it will become part of the soil in the back yard.

Our next door neighbor, the same one whose friend was pinned under the car, has a dog named Junior. Junior thought our day lily plant in the front yard needed him to water it. After so much water, the poor lily curled up and went into a long sleep. The good news is that this morning Grandpa transferred our lily to the back yard and planted a thorny rose bush to replace it in the front yard. We'll let you know how Junior likes it.

Love,

Grandma and Grandpa

54

October Thoughts

Oct 20, 05

Dear Grand Children,

Your Aunt Ann and Uncle John were born in October and isn't that a reason to celebrate? Ann has more experience with life than John, meaning she is older; is she then wiser? Canada's Thanksgiving occurs during this month and, as you know, Halloween falls on the last day, more reasons to celebrate!

The flower for the month of October is Calendula (*Calendula officinalis*), its common name is pot marigold, but it is a member of the Aster family and not related to the common garden marigold that we grow in our yards. Both Calendula and the garden marigold have bright orange and yellow flowers, so we would have to study both plants to discover the differences.

Calendula earned its name because it likes to bloom once a month or at the new moon. It is also called "poor man's saffron" because of its vibrant color and flavoring for soups, rice and chowders. The colorful petals can be added to salads.

An herb, Calendula has been cultivated in the Mediterranean area for centuries and besides growing it for food, people have used it for medicine. It soothes rashes, sunburns, chapped hands, and insect bites. This plant contains compounds that make it anti-inflammatory (reduces heat and pain), an astringent (pulls together cuts in the skin), and an antiseptic (cleansing; antibacterial and antiviral). More information about this powerful herb can be found on the internet if you search on the word *Calendula*. You will discover many uses for this plant.

If you know anything about October's birthstone, you will know that the opal is a difficult stone to identify because of its range of colors from clear through white, milky blue, gray, red, yellow, green, brown and black. Oh my! We are sure that there is an explanation for all those colors, and you can research that, too.

There is no doubt that October offers us mystery, intrigue, awe, inspiration, and surprises. Our lives are enriched by October's magic, and we become more aware that we are just one tiny part of the amazing Universe.

Be grateful for our magnificent world home, and breathe your peace, love and blessings to Aunt Ann and Uncle John.

With love to our Grand Wonders,

Grandma and Grandpa

55

From Winona to Durian to...

Oct 21, 05

Dear Grand Children

Tuesday we drove to Winona, a town on the Mississippi River, to visit St. Mary's University. A women's art exhibit had some paintings done by an old friend of ours. Each woman had a unique style, so it was easy to identify which artist created each piece of artwork.

On our short trip, we were mesmerized by the splendor of autumn colors. The variety of hues we saw ranged from yellow, gold, orange, red, fuchsia, maroon, lavender and all shades in between. The trees in our yard have all shed their leaves after last night's winds, but some of you southerners must be enjoying the visual beauty yet.

Each area has soil with nutrients common to that area, each tree has its own personal chemical make-up and appearance, and many different species of trees give us unique displays of color. Minnesota has tree stands that hold different kinds of trees, deciduous that shed their leaves each year, and coniferous trees that are evergreens and cone-bearing or that have arillate fruit. Arillate is a fleshy, usually brightly colored cover of a seed; the bright-red covering of a yew berry for example. Looking up arillate on the internet led us to an article which explained that every tree that has this kind of seed has invented a way to travel. This seed is called "fruit" but is not the kind that we would eat.

Here is what David Quammen has written about arillate

But not every fruit travels as well, or as far, as others. Some kinds are adventurous. Some are more laggard. Some hit the ground unswallowed and don't even roll.

So to get to the core of the matter, you'll need to do a little traveling yourself. Start with a flight to Bali, an island in Indonesia. Then follow your nose upwind toward a species of tree called *Durio zibethinus* (an arillate fruit.)

The fruit of that tree is big as a rugby ball and upholstered all over with thorns. It goes by the name durian, from the Malaysian word *duri*, for "thorn." It is hard and hangs from a stout stem and God help you if you're beneath when it falls. It looks about as succulent as a stuffed porcupine but splits open to reveal its amazing innards. Each inner chamber contains several large gobbets of ivory-white pulp. That's the edible stuff. Inside each gobbet is a seed. The seed itself is as big as a chestnut. Durian is renowned throughout Asia for its luxuriant flavor, its peculiar anatomy, and its indecent stench.

The seed-bearing structure travels by wind power, or by floating on water, or by catching a ride aboard an animal. According to this strict definition, the downy white parachute of a dandelion seed constitutes fruit. The whirlybird wing that carries a maple seed is a fruit. A leathery acacia pod is a fruit, and so is an acorn, and so is a burr." (From *"The Great Stinking Clue"* by David Quammen)

This letter about autumn color led to "arillate," the covering of some seeds. So now we could research "fruit." Curiosity about our world never ends!

OXOX to all our Fruit Lovers,

Grandma and Grandpa

56

Glaucoma

Nov 14, 05

Dear Grand Children,

Let's talk about "inheritance" and "heredity." Inheritance means that you possess or receive something (a piece of property like a house or land, or a quality like green eyes) from your parents. Heredity is a trait handed down from your parents. So you can inherit a trait from your parents who received it from their parents on through many generations.

Your Grandpa Mayer just discovered that he has glaucoma, a disorder of the eye and a leading cause of blindness in the United States. If it is treated early, vision loss is avoided. His mother had glaucoma and his brother Lawrence also has it. Both Grandpa and Lawrence are taking eye drops to stop the progress of glaucoma. You and your Mayer parent might have inherited this disease.

The eye is one of the magical parts of our human power engine. It is a complicated cog of our engine in which fluid circulates all around its parts. This fluid acts like lubricating oil, keeping all the parts of the eye working smoothly, and this fluid is constantly being made. When everything works right, it drains out through a tiny opening to the outer eye. If the drainage point does not function well, the fluid doesn't drain and pressure builds up within the eye

The pressure then damages the optic nerve which deteriorates and becomes impaired. Grandpa has nerve damage, but his sight is still very good. Peripheral vision, the outer edges of vision, is the first part of sight that is affected by glaucoma. Grandpa's peripheral vision is good, so you still will not be able to sneak up on him from the side.

Glaucoma begins about the time a person is 60 years old. If you have a Mayo Clinic Family Health Book, turn to page 765 for glaucoma. The next two pages have pictures of the ways vision is altered with this disease, and a diagram of the eye helps to explain this condition.

Grandpa was not happy with the news that he is a carrier of glaucoma. He would rather not be bothered with eye drops. Yet, he continues to read and write, and enjoys observing nature, so his life has changed only a little bit every night for a minute or two. You may have inherited the genes of this disease but you all have inherited some others from him that are wonderful. You all like to tease, and most of you like to sing loud, and you all have inherited some physical features – hmmmm, you might not be happy with those! Breathe him your love and peace.

I breathe love and peace to you and your parents,

Grandma

57

Thanksgiving

Nov 22, 05

Dear Grand Children,

Here we are at Thanksgiving time again, and remembering things that make us thankful. This time of year our gardens have spent their lives blooming and producing their bounty for us. Some have dropped their seeds, and already their dream for next year has been planted.

This morning Grandpa is donating blood for those who will need it soon. He is a universal blood donor, O Negative, which means anyone can be helped with this blood type. Because of that, the clinic calls him as often as they can for his donation. We are thankful that he can do this to help others.

While Grandpa was gone, Grandma tried making a little box for a gift; it is the first time she tried doing this, and ended up with a trapezoid! The next time should be better, and we are thankful we have more time to develop and enjoy skills.

We are packing to visit our family in Milwaukee, and have prepared some pumpkin pies and the apple cake that looks like a pie. We anticipate a turkey dinner tomorrow, all of it from the bounty of Earth. We are thankful for the abundance that lives and grows around us, some of that becoming our nourishment.

We are grateful, too, for you Wonders. You are masterfully made, high-energy models, with some traits from your parents and grandparents, *yet more than all of that.* We are thankful for you just the way you are!

We marvel at the variety in our lives that the Universe unfolds, and are thankful for the many doors in our Earth Home that provide us with a glimpse of our Maker.

You have many other reasons to be thankful. We know, too, that this year has had disappointments and struggle for you, but we ask you to begin each day being thankful that you are wonderfully made and that your world is full of adventure and delight. Breathe all the things that you desire for yourselves—breathe them to the world,—and add peace and harmony, healing and forgiveness if you hadn't thought of that!

We breathe you peace and love,

Grandma and Grandpa

58

No Boring Days

Dec 7, 05

Dear Grand Children,

Snow has fallen intermittently (off and on) today, the sun having a contest with the clouds, each trying to have the greater influence on our weather. Grandpa bought a snow blower the day before our first snowfall, so we have a choice about how we want to clear it away.

Grandma's back is sore from putting up Christmas decorations and wrestling with furniture; the furniture won! She is exercising so she can pick up her grand children when they come for the holidays.

We had an "open house" on Monday for two candidates who want to represent us in Congress. Mary and Bill Jenney, your great aunt and uncle from Brooklyn Center, were here to help with greeting people and keeping food on the table and punch in the bowl. We had about fifty people, not counting the candidates and their aides for the campaign. Ford Bell is running for the Senate, and Tim Walz is running for First District Representative, the same seat that Grandpa campaigned for during spring of 2004. The people who came were glad to have the opportunity to talk with the candidates and share their views on health care, education, and war in Iraq as well as other issues. Remember their names, and listen for them in November next year during the election.

On December 4, Patty became a teenager! A time of physical, mental, emotional and spiritual growth spurts, does that mean that she will shoot up in height or have an explosion of creativity or a yen for adventure? Maybe she will surprise us with all three! Her aunts and uncles survived, and Kelli is on her way through those years which can seem like a ride on a roller-coaster, so Patty will make it, too.

Tonight we will hear a long-time environmentalist from Rochester talk about how soon our oil supply will run out. The world is not yet ready with alternative renewable fuels. Europe has worked on the problem longer than the U.S. so they are developing ways to use waste products for fuel and new ways to transport products. This is a daunting (scary) time in our history, but also a very hopeful time.

As you can tell, we are not bored! Observing nature brings us curiosity and wonder; reading transports us to historical times and exotic locations; interests—old and new—entice us to participate in exciting events. We are truly blessed with the gifts of adventure, health, imagination, and family; and we breathe these gifts to you.

We love you,

Grandma and Grandpa

59

Christmas

Dec 8, 05

Dear Grand Children,

    We are in the middle of Advent, a time of remembering and a time of waiting to celebrate the birth of Jesus. What many of us don't know is how our celebration of Christmas, Jesus' birth, is connected to ancient traditions that began way before the time he was born!

    Because Jesus' birthday was not recorded in the bible or anywhere else, Julius I, who was pope in 336 A.D., declared his birthday to be December 25th,—300 years after he lived! On December 25th, Romans celebrated children and the birthday of Mithra, god of the unconquerable sun.

    Other ancient holidays during this time celebrated longer sunlight hours after the Winter Solstice, and commemorated light and birth in the darkest days of the year. In winter, German tribes honored the god Oden. Pope Julius I must have wanted to adapt these traditions that celebrate children, life and birth, and sunlight,—good reasons to have a holiday or a holyday!

    In ancient Europe, especially in the North, most cattle were slaughtered in the winter because feed for animals was scarce. Food was gathered and prepared, and with fresh meat, our ancestors took the opportunity to enjoy weeks of feasting, often with boisterous parties. They would tote home a huge log, set it on fire, and feast until the log burned out.

    By the 1550s, Christmas became the reason to celebrate, and customs that developed from ancient beliefs had become traditional. Lots of food, jolly family gatherings, and wine-drinking became Christmas customs.

Pilgrims who lived in the 1600s did not think all these customs borrowed from the ancient festivals were appropriate, so not only the customs but the Christmas holiday itself was cancelled in England, and it was against the law to celebrate Christmas in "New World" Boston for more than twenty years. In fact, Christmas was not declared a holiday in the U.S. until 1870. Our Declaration of Independence was written in 1776, so about 100 years later Christmas finally became a national holiday in our country!

It is interesting that New York City organized its first police force because of a riot during the Christmas season in 1828; this was a time when people couldn't find work and when rich merchants and their families were not concerned about those who were hungry and poor. Two authors who have influenced how we celebrate Christmas is Washington Irving who wrote "The Sketchbook of Geoffrey Crayon," and Charles Dickens who wrote "A Christmas Carol." The authors wrote about the importance of respecting all people and about caring for children. They portray Christmas as a peaceful, family-oriented and warm-hearted holiday when hearts and homes are opened to those who are less fortunate.

Jesus came to tell us that we all belong to God's family as brothers and sisters, that what we do to others we do to our Creator's family, and that peace comes when we treat each other in respectful ways. Remembering that, let us choose the best customs that celebrate this holy time.

We breathe warmth, love, and abiding peace to you and your Parents,

Grandma and Grandpa

60

Thoughts of Jesus

Dec 16, 05

Dear Grand Children,

Christmas is nearly here! We hope you are enjoying the anticipation of good things to come, and yet remember our past Christmases and treasure all that has happened.

Let's think of last year's Christmas time, or our surprise birthday party in August. You came at different times to those special days, and you each have different memories of your cousins playing with you, of aunts and uncles and grandparents talking with you. You each experienced something different, and I hope you especially remember the hugs, fun games, the wonderful tasting food, the humorous conversations.

No one wrote about Jesus until years after he died, and those writings were by people who didn't know him. But the memory of him was so etched on people's minds that they continued to tell others about his way of seeing the truth that was different from most other people. Each person saw events of Jesus' life from their own experiences, just as our memories of last Christmas are different from those who spent it with us.

What we read in the Gospels are pieces of memory that easily became exaggerated as the story of Jesus was told again and again. The gospel details differ as we read about Jesus. He may have had shepherds visit on his birth, and maybe he was born in a stable, but these details are really not important.

So what is important about Jesus? He experienced the Divine Presence in the world—in people, in nature, in all things. This is not a new idea because it is found in the Hebrew Scriptures, but what is new is that he spent his life telling everyone to recognize themselves as carriers of the Divine Presence. When we were young we were taught that we are "temples of the Holy Spirit," another way of saying that the Divine is with us. Jesus showed by his life that our Creator loved us all, not only our friends but people we consider to be our enemies, too. Violence and war were not his "weapons;" he used respect, humor, story, feasting, consolation, healing, and love as his way of bringing others to experience the Divinity in themselves.

This was not an "aha" moment that he kept to himself; no, he trumpeted the good news of Divine Presence. He wanted everyone to know that they were special carriers of their Creator. We are all equal as brothers and sisters in the family of our Creator. All that is life—our work, play, contemplation, delight, method of governing, and method of worshipping—is affected by the truth that the Divine Spirit lives within each of us.

Knowing that Divine Presence lives in each member of the global family freed Jesus to act contrary to some of the cultural taboos of his day. Women were to be seen and not heard, but Jesus spoke and spent time with women. No one was to work on the Sabbath, but Jesus would help others if they needed it, even on the Sabbath. Pharisees were the elite Jewish members who thought highly of themselves, and Jesus was not afraid to have a chat with them when he thought they could use some advice.

So how does Divine Life within ourselves free us to change? That is the question that we can ask ourselves this Christmas. It is an exciting new adventure for us to consider.

We breathe you the love and peace that Jesus was born to bring to us,

Grandma and Grandpa

61

Luke's Baptism

Dec 18, 05

Dear Grand Children,

Today is special because Luke was baptized this morning. The baptism began before the liturgy, with an anointing (blessing) of oil, signing him with a cross on his forehead which we all were invited to do.

After the homily, we went to the large font of water and Father Mahon, who assisted at Jen and Lee's wedding, poured water over Luke's forehead to show the world that he is special to God and to us. Others who gathered around the font then had a chance to mark him with the sign of the cross.

We all, the Greseth grandparents, Godparents and other relatives and friends came to our house for a big lunch. This is the prayer we said then:

> Spirit of the Universe, before the beginning of time, you created our world and called it, all of it, good. Before the beginning of time, you called Luke by name, and he is yours. Wherever he ventures on his life journey you are with him because he is precious in your sight and you love him with an everlasting love.
>
> Holy Wisdom, we can glimpse your generous love in the smiles and chatter of Luke who mirrors your delight in the unfolding Universe. With awe, we too are drawn to the miracle of life that continues to surround us and bless us.

Creator of Life, we thank you for Jen and Lee, for their commitment to love and care for Luke, to provide direction and encouragement as he explores his inner and outer universe. We thank you for all the blessings you lavish on them, your blessings always there, theirs to take up.

Extravagant Love, we thank you for Luke's Godparents,—Sherri, Scott, and Mary—for their willingness to find opportunities for Luke's spiritual growth. We thank you for this Christian community which welcomes Luke as a follower of Jesus, your son who begs all of us to be his brothers and sisters in the family of God.

Holy One, everything is holy because it all comes from you. We discover your life and holiness in creatures large and small, in plants and in the soil that nurtures them, in Luke and in ourselves, in the constellations you scatter through space. We are filled with wonder at the goodness and holiness that surrounds us, and we bow our heads and bend our knees in gratitude.

Amen.

We breathe you love and serenity,

Grandma and Grandpa

Jen & Lee

Luke & Morgan in the rain

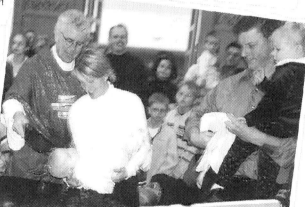

Luke's Baptism

Mary & Bill Jenney

Steve & Leanna the Great

62

New Year's and Recycling

Dec 31, 05

Dear Grand Children,

On the last day of the year, it is raining in Rochester. We have not had a freezing temperature for two weeks, and as much as we don't like to admit it, we miss the snow! Some people attribute our unusual weather to global warming or el Niño, but others tell us it is a natural development and "get over it."

Whether there is a reason or not for global warming, all of us need to take care of the world in which we live and play. We are sure that in school you are told to "recycle, reuse, and restore;" those are the three Rs of the environment, and important like reading, riting and rithmetic. Hmmm, maybe we should add rspelling to that list.

How many ways do you know that will help us conserve water? Connor and Eamon had some experience with that last summer when they were living on the farm with no running water and no faucets. Of course, they may not have had the opportunity to take showers as often as their cousins, unfortunate for those who lived with them. Do you know how they showered?

How many ways can you use paper sacks and plastic bags to give them a second life? Ours are used for garbage and some are returned to the grocery stores, and we take the plastic bags to an organic food store. The heavy cloth bags your parents received for Christmas are for bringing home groceries and for library books, so remind your parents to take it along when they shop or go to the library. We have found that sometimes grocery baggers don't feel comfortable using them, and we have to suggest that they fill our cloth bags before they reach for any other kind.

To conserve our car and the gas it takes to run it, we walk and occasionally bike, but have never skateboarded or taken the bus to go anywhere. It has been a looonnnggg time since we ran anywhere! We need exercise especially as we get older, so walking to go downtown is part of our efforts for a healthier lifestyle. This year, we will be investigating and using the city buses for getting around town.

What are your suggestions for taking care of our environment? We challenge you to experiment with some of them. You may think that taking care of the places where you live is not enough to make a difference in our world, but it all helps. We each can do a little better, and you will be an example for others. Let us know your suggestions to this challenge!

Love and blessings for the New Year,

Grandma and Grandpa

63

Triskaidekaphobia

Jan 13, 06

Dear Grand Children,

Today is Friday the thirteenth! If I were superstitious (afraid of something because I don't understand it or give it importance that it doesn't have) I would be very careful today. I would not walk under a ladder, but I wouldn't do that on any day. I didn't stay inside to avoid any bad luck, either. When I worked at the Clinic library, the 13th floor was not open to the public; it housed all the utility pipes and maintenance materials for the building, and I'm sure that it was because many people are superstitious about the number thirteen.

Triskaidekaphobes (trisk eye DECK uh fobes) are people who have an irrational (unreasonable) fear of the number thirteen. It may seem unlucky to them, but not to professional counselors who charge them a fee for treating their malady. (One chuckle permitted here.) Actually, counselors teach Triskaidekaphobes how to focus on pleasant thoughts. Our ability to train ourselves to dwell on happy and positive thoughts gets us through life a little easier, and some of us who suffer from phobias (FOH bee ahs; a person who has an irrational or exaggerated fear of something) sometimes need help in learning that skill.

This has been a good day, in spite of this day that gets a bad rap from triskaidekaphobes. We stopped at the library and checked out some good books, ate delicious meals, visited with a friend, and are listening to soothing music. And we are planning to visit Jackson and his family for a few days next week. How can we not be grateful for these blessings?

Breathe your peace and love to those who have irrational and unhealthy fears, and you will bring serenity to them and to the global family as well. It is a scientific fact!

Love and oxoxox,

Grandma

64

Genome

Jan 25, 06

Dear Grand Children,

Genome (JEN ohm). Are you familiar with that word? A Genome carries all the information from your parents that determines your height, sex, hair color, shape of fingernails etc. etc. etc.

The genome is like a book, but it is a tiny book because it is located in the nucleus of most of your cells. A cell is so tiny that it can fit on the top of a pinhead!

Each nucleus in this tiny cell has two genomes, one from each of your parents. The genome book has 23 *chromosomes* or chapters. In each chapter are thousands of stories called *genes*, and each story is made up of paragraphs. The words in these paragraphs use three letters, but the book's alphabet has only four letters. The genome/ book in each cell is constantly being read and copied. Are you confused yet?

So what's the point? It is a mystery how that pair of genomes can fit into such a space and yet function to keep us alive and working. It is a mystery how they combine into our own book. As you can imagine, with so many stories (genes), many things can go wrong; a misspelled word can change the story enough for a dreadful mistake to occur so that we would experience a disease or handicap, or the misspelled word may not matter at all in our story. There is so much to read in our genome that scientists are scrambling with enthusiasm to unravel the secrets that are found there. They already have discovered that our genes have recorded important events in our development; the genome is an autobiography with stories of our relationships and connections that can be traced all the way back to primitive worms that inhabited the primeval (first) ooze of young Earth.

The genome will give up its secrets eventually, but will that be the last word in revealing all there is to know about life? Hardly. There is much more to learn about the genome, but even if we learned everything about it, would we be able to explain our thoughts and dreams? How does the genome interact with our thoughts and emotions and physical bodies? Can we anticipate how and when genes will change as our world continues to unfold and develop? Sometimes we are aware of changes but most often they happen so slowly that we do not have a clue!

We live in a marvelous world; we belong to a mysterious web of relationships; we are connected to ancient creation which continues its unfolding even today. We are amazed by it, and grateful that you are part of this Beautiful Design which the Divine Creator has launched.

Oh, and for your information, 98 percent of chimpanzee genes match human genes. 97 percent of both chimpanzee and human genes match apes' genes, so chimpanzees are more closely related to humans than to apes!

We breathe you peace and love,

Grandma and Grandpa

65

Things that Can't be Bought

Feb 2, 06

Dear Grand Children,

Snow dust is gracefully swirling from the rooftops, sparkling in the sun, a welcome change from yesterday's dreary drizzly darkness. How's that for alliteration? (words that begin with the same letter or sound) These snowflake diamonds catch the light as you fling them up in the air, but the diamonds are a surprise when they happen—you just have to keep your eyes open as nature works its magic.

From our front window we watch the squirrels bound along their highway from our big fir tree to the tall bushes along the side of our house. They lunge to the rooftop and continue to the large Maple by the back corner of our house where they drop to the fence and scamper all the way to the end of our lot. Would they be surprised if we were to trim up some of their highway? After moving to this house, one of the first things we did was trim our trees, and then we noticed the squirrels pacing back and forth on the neighbor's roof, trying to figure out what happened to their highway. It was very comical to us, but probably not to the squirrels.

Some of the best things that have happened to us are the surprises from nature, the beauty we encounter in a sunset or a walk in a park, the visits we enjoy with you and your families. These things can't be bought.

When we were growing up, did we notice all the subtleties, things that are not-in-your-face, of nature? No. Do we have more time to take to observe them now? We think we are as busy as we ever were, but it must be that we have become better observers and pay closer attention to the natural world around us. Our Earth Garden is a cathedral, a holy place where we have a choice of doorways to the Spirit of the Universe who is in all of Creation,—plants, animals, earth, air, water, humans, galaxies, and beyond everything that we know.

Our Cosmic Dreamer had you in mind before the beginning of time, before the birth of the Universe billions of years ago. You are ancient because nothing has been added to the Universe in all those years! You are young, too, because you are part of the transformation and emergence that is happening to the soup and dust and elements from that first flowering of the Universe. You are precious, more precious than you can imagine. The Cosmic Dreamer has imprinted your hearts and enclosed in every cell of your body the love, the life-spark, and the yearning to know about the stuff of which you are made.

Love to our precious Dreamers,

Grandma and Grandpa

66

Food and Sacrament

Feb 4, 06

Dear Grand Children,

Do you have a favorite food or snack? Lately, we have really enjoyed mixing peanuts with candy corn to make a treat that reminds us of salted nut rolls. We can OD on them, well, maybe just Grandma. The candy seems to disappear faster than the peanuts. We don't know if stores sell salted nut rolls anymore because we never look for them.

The pleasure of tasting foods is taken for granted most of the time because it has always been available for us. We are really privileged to never have to worry about getting enough to eat. We can buy a variety of foods at grocery stores, and some of you are lucky enough to have food from your very own gardens. You may never have experienced real hunger.

Our ancestors used to forage, (hunt for berries and roots) for their meals. Then they learned to cultivate the things they enjoyed eating. These plants are gifts from Mother Earth, and our earliest grandparents knew that products of the soil were imagined by the Cosmic Spirit who made it possible for them to develop for our enjoyment and nourishment. How food becomes our energy and transforms us from babies through all the changes in our lives is a mystery. Plants develop and repair us, and waste products—including our own (no yuks here, please)—become the food for plants, a cycle of birth and growth and death to birth again.

The Creator of the Universe encloses the life-spark—or Divinity—in everything, so what we eat is not only food but also a gift that contains that mark of life and holiness. People today who have maintained a connection to ancient beliefs have a deep reverence for nature because, for them, the Spirit is found within everything in the Universe, including food.

For these early people, it was natural to show their appreciation for the gifts of food and taste that they enjoyed. They would thank the spiritual protector of the animals for the "favor" of killing the animal to eat. They were grateful for the animal and yet sorry that a "hole" was temporarily made in the fabric of the universe.

Today, we mimic our ancestors when we recognize by a prayer or whisper of breath that sister plants and brother animals are gifts from the Spirit of the Universe. This blessing or grace of holy food is a "sign" of our Creator's love for us, and we thank the Compassionate Spirit for this gift.

Grateful for you, the greatest of our "signs" of Divine love,

Grandma and Grandpa

67

Last Supper

Feb 12, 06

Dear Grand Children,

We wrote recently about the lavish variety of plants in our Earth Garden. These plants are saturated with Divine Life and are a sign of the Cosmic Dreamer's love for us. We can sense—with our sight, sound, taste, feel, and smell—this extravagant love in Creation. Does this sum up our last letter?

Your parents were taught about another way of searching for God as a Catholic/ Christian follower of Christ. It is unlike our ancient grandparents who recognized God in all of nature and believed that nature was a beautiful gift or grace. That grace was there for everyone, but today, churches have priests or ministers who have become responsible for bringing some of these gifts to the members of their communities.

Christian churches have developed ceremonies around some gifts called sacraments which come to us out of God's abundant love. A sacrament is a sign of God's grace or gift to us. Some churches recognize the two sacraments of Baptism and Communion; some also recognize the sacrament of Confirmation. The Catholic tradition has four other sacraments; Matrimony, Penance, Sacrament of the Sick, and Holy Orders.

Matrimony is a church sacrament that is given by the wedding couple to each other; the priest or minister is only a witness just as we who attend are witnesses to the couple as they pledge their love and devotion to each other.

We assume that a priest or minister must be on hand for a sacrament (gift) to come to us, but that is not true, and there are hundreds of gifts that church leaders have not made into ceremonies. Those gifts are ours whenever we reach out for them. They can be our visits or fun with friends, planting and tending a garden, swimming, reading, playing music or hearing birdsong, tasting foods, touching a furry gerbil. The Creator's gifts come to us through our senses in which everything can be experienced. Because our experiences send information to our hearts and minds, gifts also come in the form of forgiveness, love, acceptance, humor, and gratitude, and we know you will be able to name more of them!

The Eucharist, or Communion, is a ritual to remember the "Last Supper" when Jesus celebrated the Jewish feast of the Passover with his friends. The Passover honors the time that Jews were saved from Egyptian slavery. At this meal he blessed and divided the food and gave it to those around the table. He said "This is my body, this is my blood; do this to remember me." Some Christians believe that we actually eat and drink his body and blood; others believe the importance of it is to remember what happened at that meal. To most people, it doesn't matter what others believe about communion; they all receive it as a Divine gift and a sign of God's care and love for us.

It is not difficult to think about the bread and wine as "body and blood" if we have the same awe and wonder that our ancestors had for all Creation. They believed that we,—along with our cousin plants, sister stars, and brother animals—were one Universe, a holy web of life united with our Creator. In this web, we then participate in communion every time we eat.

We breathe peace and love to our Web partners,

Grandma and Grandpa

68

Tragedy

Feb 12, 06

Dear Grand Children,

Last evening tragedy hit our neighborhood. Three houses to the east of us, we noticed a Fire Rescue van driving away, and four or five police cars parked along the front. One of our neighbors called us about it because he had been curious and went over to talk to a policeman who was circling the yard with yellow tape, but our neighbor wasn't told anything about what happened.

About 10:30 in the evening, a detective knocked on our door and told us a man who lived in that house had died and the police were looking for his adult son. He wanted to know whether we saw a red Impala earlier in the day, or whether we knew the people from that house. We hadn't seen the car, and the residents were never outside when we could have seen them. The man who died was the son of the old folks who used to live there. All night a police car was parked there, probably to dissuade any curious people from going beyond the tape.

This morning, TV news stations arrived and were taking pictures and knocking on neighborhood doors for interviews. A young woman from an area TV station came to our house and wanted to know whether we were afraid. We said no because the crime seemed to stem from a family issue. We both told her that we believe this is a miniature example of the way our country deals with disagreements, which is to strike before even talking over the problem. The New York Times reported today that violent crime rose sharply in 2005 compared to 2004 in larger cities, and mentioned Milwaukee as one of the cities. It is easier to buy handguns now, and arguments that shouldn't even come to a fist-fight are ending up as a violent crime. We don't think our remarks will be mentioned in their news report because we declined to be interviewed on camera.

A Bureau of Criminal Apprehension vehicle has been parked on the street today, along with other vans, probably more police personnel.

Some painful events must have led to such a dreadful act for this family. That person who committed the crime will never be free from last night's nightmare. We don't know whether it is the son, but this is speculation from what the detective told us. We have learned from the local TV news this evening that someone who was found in the Twin Cities area is in custody. Whoever committed the crime has a lifetime to deal with the horror of it.

Breathe your peace and love to neighborhoods, yours and ours; and breathe peace, healing and love to the family that is burdened with this awful sorrow.

Love to our Breathing Healers,

Grandma and Grandpa

69

Eats, Shoots and Leaves

Feb 17, 06

Dear Grand Children,

What does the title of the book, *Eats, Shoots and Leaves*, conjure up in your mind? This little book looks humorously at wrong punctuation, so that is a clue.

Lynn Truss, the British woman who wrote the book, goes bananas when commas, quotes, or apostrophes are not used appropriately. She has seen grocery stores with signs that read "orange,s apple.s and grape,s" in their fruit sections. She cringes when she is confronted with "Ladie's Hairdresser" and "Mens coat's." She develops a gut-ache when "XMA'S TREES" are advertised.

Without proper punctuation, the meaning of a sentence can be 180 degrees wrong. For example—"A woman, without her man, is nothing"; or "A woman: without her, man is nothing"

A story is told that in a performance of the play *Hamlet* by Shakespeare, a soldier was calling for help for his wounded comrade and he cheerfully calls out "Go get him, surgeons!" It was supposed to be "Go, get him surgeons!" I'm not sure the director of the play would really let that happen.

Lynn is a "closet paparazzi" who arms herself with correction fluid, big pens, stickers in a variety of sizes for covering up unwanted apostrophes, a tin of paint, guerilla-style clothing, and as a last resort, she packs a gun. (I think this is supposed to be humorous here.) She and those like her who have a problem with accepting the wrong uses of punctuation call themselves "sticklers".

A former editor and sports columnist who now writes novels, she reviews books and occasionally is interviewed on BBC radio. "Eats,

Shoots and Leaves" is a bestseller so we brought it home from the library because we were curious about it; how can a book about a dull topic be so successful? Well, she pokes fun, has some entertaining historical information, and it is delightful to read.

The picture on the cover of the book has two pandas; one is on the ladder with a paint brush covering the comma in the title, and the other is walking off the page with a gun in its hand.

Here's the story. A panda walks into a café. He orders a sandwich, eats it, then draws a gun and fires two shots in the air. "Why did you do that?" asks the confused waiter as the panda walks towards the exit. The panda has a pamphlet on wildlife and tosses it over his shoulder. "I'm a panda," he says, at the door. "Look it up." The waiter turns to the entry on pandas and, sure enough, finds an explanation.

"**Panda**. Large black-and-white bear-like mammal, native to China. Eats, shoots and leaves."

Our love,

Grandma and Grandpa

70

Segways

Feb 25, 06

Dear Grand Children,

Have you ever seen a Segway? Another word, *segue,* is pronounced the same (SEG way) and comes from the French verb *seguire* which means to follow. A musical segue is going from one composition into another without a pause. Maybe the intention of a Segway is the same, going from one place to another without a pause. Or maybe not!

A Segway is a two-wheeled vehicle with a platform between the wheels where the person stands and holds onto handle bars that are attached to the platform with a metal column. When you ride it, you lean forward and it moves forward; when you lean backward, it takes you backward. Segways are light-weight and the steering columns collapse so that they are easy to store and handle. To see a picture of them, type it into a web search.

You may be wondering how you would ride on something like this without falling off. It has an internal balance system that works like a gyroscope with a computer to tell it how fast to move so that when you lean forward you don't fall flat on your face! It also uses a battery that plugs into an ordinary wall outlet; the Segway runs for six to thirty-six miles, depending on the model, before it has to be recharged. And they would be a blast to ride!

Rochester has purchased a Segway to use in collecting money from the parking meters, but we haven't seen it yet. Some cities are using them in police work, and some manufacturers find them efficient in moving materials. Workers enjoy using them, you would have guessed that. A special golf Segway has a metal carrier on the side for the golf bag.

But there are some problems with owning one. How do you hang on to an umbrella in the rain? Where do you park it? Is there a way to lock it? How fast will it go? Does it do donuts on ice?

This is an adventure into a new way of transportation, one that doesn't use fossil fuels unless your electricity is produced with coal. It takes about 20 cents of electricity to recharge the battery.

We should conserve our gas; we are using it so fast that the world's supply probably won't last your lifetime, and it pollutes the environment. Your parents would save on gas by installing exercise bikes in the back seats and attaching them to their car engines. That way you could generate power for the car and get your exercise at the same time! If you are hesitating on that idea, you could dream up some other solutions.

We breathe peace and love to our Dreamers,

Grandma and Grandpa

71

Shrove Tuesday

Mar 3, 06

Dear Grand Children,

Sunday we were at St. Stephen's parish in Minneapolis. Some people came to church wearing gaily colored clothes and masks, and some wore gaudy beads, even the men. Mardi Gras usually happens on Tuesday before Ash Wednesday but they were celebrating it early. We stayed for their pancake breakfast after the liturgy and enjoyed a Hispanic band which played and taught some simple dances. Part of their festivities was a silent auction—gift certificates, bird seed, soaps, art supplies, chocolate, stuffed animals and lots of other things. All were wrapped in different styles of baskets.

We didn't realize that pancakes with many different toppings are traditional meals on Shrove Tuesday until recently. Sometimes it is called Fat Tuesday, or Mardi Gras for you French scholars. It is called this because years ago, people tried to use up fat, oil, butter and other perishables before they began the forty days of fasting during Lent. They also might have wanted to use up their perishables because that is what was left of their winter supplies, and fat products can become rancid (smell bad and taste terrible).

Shrove is a very old word, and comes from the verb shrive. Its Latin root is 'scribe,' meaning to write, to write down, to prescribe, and eventually it meant to prescribe penance. So in medieval times it meant going to confession and receiving pardon for sins. Maybe that is another reason to celebrate the day before Ash Wednesday,—they felt reassured that their sins were forgiven.

A legend (story which may or may not be true) is told of a woman who was making pancakes to use up her perishable items on Shrove

146

Tuesday. She heard the church bells announcing the shriving ceremony and ran out of her thatch-roofed house, still wearing her apron and clutching the frying pan with pancakes. This supposedly occurred in England in 1445. Ever since then there have been races with frying pans and pancakes, some of them to raise money, some to just have fun. One race has the winner getting a kiss from the church's bell-ringer. You would have to know the bell-ringer to want to win that race, we think.

We are into another season of Lent and anticipating spring, the renewal and reawakening of life in our corner of Earth Garden. Our spirits are reawakening too, as winter sheds its cloak for the magical and refreshing restoration of our budding sister plants, when our animal brothers quicken their pace, and when our mysterious cousin air that we can't see and can't live without becomes a warm breath. And through this spring magic we glimpse the Spirit who cherishes us and leads us to more discoveries of our universe and of ourselves.

Love and peace to our Discoverers,

Grandma and Grandpa

72

Chaos

Mar 13, 06

Dear Grand Children,

Chaos. (*KAY-oss,* meaning confusion, disorder.) How do we explain an imperfect Universe and imperfect lives? In our wonder-filled Earth Garden we find noxious plants. We know owls consume small rodents, and rain erodes mountains. We understand these as part of nature.

Another kind of chaos occurs in our human family. We know that even something as unimportant as the color of a room can lead to disagreement. Sometimes huge disagreements develop into angry arguments, and sometimes angry arguments become war.

Our ancient grandparents looked at the chaos in their lives, the destruction and terror and war that happened to them, and believed that their gods were angry with them. Even today, many people believe that if something awful happens to them, God is angry with them. If people lived in peace and had enough to eat, they believed their God was rewarding them for being good. Today, many people believe that if you are good you will be rewarded with wealth, and if you are not good, you will be poor. This is blaming God for our personal and community problems. Read on!

Our ancestors who wrote the Old Testament thought that their God was angry with them if they lost a tribal war, so they searched for the reasons why their lives were heavy with sorrow, and they thought, "If we were to change what we eat, that would satisfy our God." And so our Old Testament relatives added more and more rules to their lives, believing that following their rules on food and cleanliness would bring favors and blessings from their God.

Some of those rules were very good. They washed their hands often; for them it was not only cleansing the body, but also the inner person. This frequent washing of hands was what saved most of them from dying during the "Black Plague" in 15th century in Europe. We know now that illness-causing germs are carried on our hands and spread to others by our touch, but we didn't know that until Florence Nightingale looked for the reason why so many English military were dying during the Crimean War in 1853 and until Louis Pasteur discovered that there really were germs that caused illness.

The stories of a wrathful god, of a god who punishes bad people, can be found in the Old Testament—also called Hebrew Scriptures—and filtered into the New Testament because that is how our ancestors explained the chaos in their lives. But there is the story of another God in the Old and New Testament, the One who holds us in the "palm of my hand," the One who calls us brothers and sisters in the global family, the One who tells us that we should treat others as we want to be treated, the One who loves us with an everlasting love. This God is with us in our happy *and* sad times, in peace *and* chaos.

This Divine Spirit, who created the Universe and found it good, expects us to *use our hearts and hands to take care of Earth Garden* and everything in it. We are the ones to bring healing and forgiveness to neighbors and classmates, to those we don't like as well as to our close friends. One way we can do this right now is by breathing in to change our fears and dark thoughts, and breathing out peace and healing. Our Global Family and Earth Garden needs *you* to nurture them in this way.

Peace and love,

Grandma and Grandpa

73

Unfairness

Mar 14, 06

Dear Grand Children,

You know all about sadness and unfairness because you have experienced them. Some sad feelings are worse than others, and unfairness is very hard to tolerate.

This is a true story. A man is in prison. He was accused of killing his wife, and a jury of twelve people decided that he was guilty, believing that the prosecutor had enough evidence against him. However, the judge didn't think the evidence was clear that he committed the murder, so the judge gave the man a short prison sentence of ten years. Now the man will be released early because of his good behavior.

The man's aunt tells us that he is innocent of the crime. Can you imagine how he must have felt all those years in prison? The person who did commit the murder is free, and the nephew lost his job and was denied some good years with his family. The nephew also wondered where God was when he needed to feel that Divine love, that love which flows throughout the Universe. We know that our Loving Creator is with the nephew in his prison years, even though he felt disconnected.

How can we explain the unfair trial and its terrible consequences for his whole life? We each make choices and those choices affect the people we live with. Choice is a gift of our Cosmic Dreamer. This gift is magnificent and dangerous, and when we make choices to benefit others, then we benefit ourselves, too. You will remember times when this doesn't work; this gift is not an easy one to use well. The real criminal's actions ruined many lives, and the nephew has a life to rebuild.

It is difficult for any of us to believe that our Creator loves the guilty person as much as the nephew. It is difficult to offer forgiveness and healing equally to both of them, because we think that one deserves it and the other does not. It is very difficult to love our enemies, but Jesus tells us to love them because we all belong to God's family. This love and forgiveness is possible when we remember that the Source, the Spirit, of love and forgiveness is within and around each of us.

You must be wondering what we can do for the nephew. The best we can do is to breathe peace, love, forgiveness and healing. Breathe it to the nephew, the guilty person, the jury and all those who had a part in the trial. Our Earth Garden needs much healing, and you are the miracles that will make it happen.

Love to our Miracle-Workers,

Grandma and Grandpa

74

Reconciliation

Mar 15, 06

Dear Grand Children,

The last two letters you received from us have been about God's love for everyone; we are brothers and sisters in the one global family of God. When we become hurt, it is not because our Creator has destined us for pain; we may never know in this life why we suffer, but we—or others in our human family—may have caused it, sometimes unknowingly.

You already know that our choices can be hurtful to ourselves and others, and sometimes that pain is terrible. The Spirit of the Universe has a huge heart of love and compassion that enfolds us all, which we especially need to remember in our worst times. Two things should happen in order to heal. We need to ask forgiveness for our bad decisions and the hurt we have caused, and we need to accept the apologies for the bad decisions and harm others have caused us.

What if the person or persons you have hurt do not want to talk to you and will not accept your apology? You can go to a parent or school counselor for advice. You may also want to talk over some problems you have that come from the actions of other people.

The Catholic Church has a sacrament called *Reconciliation* in which you confide your mistakes to a priest who will help you find solutions and lay your problems to rest. After this sacrament, many people feel that they have unloaded their burdens and find God's presence and healing within it; some people have not found it satisfying and don't often use it. Other Christian churches don't have this sacrament, but their pastors are counselors and will help you work on your problems.

When we regret a choice we have made and try to mend the pain we have caused, we meet the Spirit of the Universe whose presence and healing is there for us, no matter how we seek to correct our mistakes—in asking forgiveness from the person we hurt, or in the sacrament of Reconciliation, or in counseling, or in all of these ways.

We also meet the Spirit of the Universe when we accept an apology by someone who asks our forgiveness! Forgiving someone can be more difficult than asking a person to forgive us. We need to learn how to forgive others without accepting their painful action as being ok.

Corrie Ten Boom wrote "The Hiding Place" about how her family in Holland hid Jews during World War II. They were caught at it, and sent to concentration camps where her sister and father died. Her book, "Tramp for the Lord," is about her life after being freed, and tells of a time when she was in the same room with the cruelest camp guard she ever had in the concentration camps. This was the last person she wanted to see. She prayed fervently to be able to forgive him and wrote, *"For a long moment we grasped each other's hands, the former guard and the former prisoner. I had never known God's love so intensely as I did then."* Her forgiveness was possible because she connected to God and transferred God's love and healing to her enemy.

Was it also a moment when she experienced the love of the Creator from her enemy? We guess that it may have happened that way. She wrote that other war victims who could forgive were best able to rebuild their lives. Forgiveness can be difficult, but it makes healing easier.

Love to our Healing and Forgiving Breathers,

Grandma and Grandpa

75

San Diego Trip

Apr 1, 06

Dear Grand Children,

The third week in March we were in San Diego to visit your Uncle Joe and his family, a great time for us. We were not ready to return to chilly Minnesota weather although this is the rainy season in southern California.

Your Uncle Joe's lemon and orange trees were loaded again with fruit. With the lemon juice he has stored in his freezer we had lemonade every day, a treat we remember from last year.

We spent Sunday at the La Jolla (*lah HOY-ah*) coast, north of San Diego. Seals use part of a secluded inlet—most of the time it is a beach area for us humans—for their nursery, so we saw some young pups cavorting in the waves, daring to go a little further each time, but the moms were keeping careful watch. Some older scruffier seals were basking in the sun in a rocky area where the ocean spewed and sprayed (alliteration here!) them. They might have liked it there because that sprinkler system kept them cool.

The day Kelli and JD left San Diego with their Mother for some skiing, we went to the desert with your Uncle Joe, Molly and her two children, Buddy and Caitie. Buddy reluctantly joined us, claiming that "if you see one rock, you see them all." It was a rocky walk in the desert, some boulders as big as utility sheds piled together as if a monstrous mechanical claw dropped them there.

An arroyo, which is a riverbed or streambed that is dry most of the year except in the rainy season, wound its way through the desert, and along this arroyo was the smoothest path. It contained some water because of the recent rain. Longhorn sheep were splashing and drinking from it at one deeper spot. Palm tree trunks marked the path where rushing water spilled out of the mountains and widened the arroyo. Sometimes we had to climb over trunks that were 20 inches in diameter. If you make a circle with your arms, you would make the size of a smaller trunk.

After an hour's trek, we reached a spot where coyotes "planted" some palm tree seeds. The oasis which grew there was very cool under the shelter of those palms, and we put on our sweaters. Some of the oasis area is fenced off to provide a place for young sprouts to take root, but we didn't see any new growth. This is where the trees were uprooted and started their journey along the arroyo. We would not like to get caught there when heavy rainfall collects from the mountains and rushes down into a raging, threatening, out-of-control wall.

Delicate blooms were peeking at us along the path, although we were three weeks too early for the best time to see the flowering desert. There is so much to see and visit in every part of our Earth Garden, and this spot has its own charm.

With love to our Wonders,

Grandma and Grandpa

In San Diego

Joe and Molly

Kelli & JD at the top; Patty,
Tim & Caroline in our backyard

Kelli, Buddy, JD and Caitie

September 28, 2007

76

Good News

Apr 21, 06

Dear Grand Children,

We have some very good news!

You may remember that two years ago, on June 14, 2004, Grandpa withdrew from his campaign to become a representative in U. S. Congress for people in southern Minnesota. This disappointed many people who had come to know him as he traveled the district he would have represented.

He had no choice but withdraw. He was experiencing balance problems and lack of energy. He had to take frequent naps.

Grandpa went through Mayo Clinic that summer and again last year. The clinic doctors found other physical problems and took care of them, but couldn't find the cause of his balance problems. He was a puzzle to the neurology doctors! On our own, we tried different diets; the hardest one to follow was the one with no gluten which is found in wheat. So he tried eating without ordinary bread, pasta, and cereal. We made weird-tasting things out of rice flour. None of that helped.

Three weeks ago your Aunt Mary Beth Weidner emailed us with some information about Meniere's disease. We had heard of it but didn't know much about it. People who suffer from this have the same symptoms of balance problems and lack of energy, but they can become worse. Sometimes their symptoms are caused by too much salt in the diet.

If you have watched Grandpa eat watermelon and cantaloupe, you know he adds salt. He lavished salt on his food, the saltier, the better. I never saw him add it to candy, though.

Three days after he quit adding salt, his balance problems ended. He has had some stressful days since then, but the stress didn't cause balance problems. We are so happy to have found a solution, and very grateful to you for breathing peace, love and healing to us.

If there is a moral to the story—a lesson to be learned—it is that there can be too much of a good thing. We can have too much candy, too much broccoli, too much sun, too many chores, and I know you can name more.

With good news there is some bad news. Grandpa is ornerier, doesn't do what he is told without asking lots of questions, and I suspect he will tease more, too. We'll just keep a salt shaker handy to sprinkle on him when he needs to mellow out!

Love to our Breathing Wonders,

Grandma

77

Earth Day

Apr 23, 06

Dear Grand Children,

More than twenty-five years ago, a man returned from the Vietnam War to his family who lived near Seattle, Washington. He was suffering from war wounds, physical and mental, having battle wounds and terrifying flashbacks that needed healing. On returning he had his ailments checked by a physician. He was given four months to live, and the doctor recommended that he find something to occupy himself that would be satisfying.

At the edge of his property was a stream. It had become the dumping ground for the neighborhood, and it was laden with garbage and toxic materials. He decided to clean it up. One of the first things he did was pull a refrigerator out of the murky stream. He thought it would kill him, but instead it made him feel better!

By observing that area while he worked on cleaning up the stream, he discovered that *mushrooms can clean toxic soil*! The longer he worked the better he felt. Other people joined him, and eventually over many years, they restored several streams along a river that empties into Puget Sound.

These people found that in taking care of Mother Earth, we take care of ourselves. We are connected. What we do to our Earth Garden affects us—how we feel and how healthy we become. In working together, we not only share the company of others and possibly make new friends, but we share the joy and blessings of our efforts.

Yesterday may have been called Earth Day, but every Day is Earth Day. In this springtime, watch the leaves turn shades of red and green as they continue to change color until they mature into their summer display, a miracle unfolding before us. We need these daily miracles so we need to take care of our Earth Garden.

What Happened to the man in Seattle, you're wondering? He, John Beal, continues to spread his healing and caring for Mother Earth. His story can be found by searching on <u>Yes Magazine.</u> That is also the place to look for more about mushrooms and their power to restore an area to health. Try searching on <u>mushroom power.</u>

Love and peace to our Healers,

Grandma and Grandpa

78

Beautiful Hand

May 12, 06

Dear Grand Children,

It has been three weeks since I broke the two fingers on my left hand, the ones closest to the thumb. So I am typing with the right hand and the left thumb, very awkward.

Coming home from downtown, I was opening the car door when I stumbled and kerplunked to the street. A young man who was in a parking lot on the other side of the street heard my keys fall to the ground and when he looked over, I was sprawled on the pavement. Being my angel of the day, he drove me to the hospital emergency room, and by that time my body was telling me that it was not at all happy with me. All of the people in the Emergency Room gave me great care and set a temporary cast. The next day, I had surgery to put pins in my fingers to hold them together until they mended.

The x-rays showed some arthritis, but also thin bones. A bone density test confirmed severe osteoporosis (thin and weak bones), so in a way it was fortunate that I have only two broken fingers. The medical remedy for osteoporosis is a medicine that requires the person to take one pill once a week one hour before breakfast. I'm not eager to take that medicine, but it will be an easy remedy.

Rochester's milk sales got bumped up since I heard that news, because milk is rich in calcium, a bone-builder, and I'm drinking lots of it now. Added to pasteurized milk is vitamin D which is needed to process calcium for the body. Protein is also needed for strong and healthy bones, but getting too much of it draws calcium away. We are a very complicated living machine!

We are also a very beautiful machine. X-rays of my hand showed the intricate and graceful bones which we all have. I also became aware of how the bones and ligaments of the hand are inter-connected, and when one part of the hand hurts, it involves other parts of the hand. That interconnection is how everything in the universe works; one thing in nature relies on many other things.

Exercise also is important for healthy bones. In the last six years, I haven't done as much walking or exercise. I thought I had done enough of that for the rest of my life!

Complicated, beautiful and magical—that describes our fingers and hands. To take care of them, we need calcium and vitamin D, and eating a balanced diet with fruits and vegetables. Walk and exercise, too. So take care of yourselves. And breathe healing my way, please.

With love to our Magical Munchkins,

Grandma

79

Grandpa's Sis Teresa

May 21, 06

Dear Grand Children,

Grandpa's sister, Teresa, is dying. Three weeks ago she suffered a stroke in which blood stops flowing to the brain or when bleeding occurs there. Now she is paralyzed on her left side and unable to speak. Abnormalities on her brain and lung also were detected. She hears and nods a reply if you ask her questions that can be answered with "yes" or "no," and she grimaces at bad jokes. In intensive care, she was hooked up with tubes to feed and medicate her and she was getting extra oxygen.

In a nursing home now, she has indicated that she doesn't want to be fed intravenously (through a tube that is strung into her vein) and doesn't want extra oxygen. She is on her way to a new life.

She is being visited by a hospice nurse who has walked this journey to new life with others. The nurse bathes Teresa, shampoos her hair, and keeps her comfortable and relaxed. Her voice is soothing and her hands tenderly care for Teresa. If we all were given that precious healing care throughout our lifetimes we would have a better world and no reason for war.

We visited with Teresa on Tuesday. She looked beautiful, no wrinkles that had lined her sixty-two-year-old face the past few years. Grandpa talked to her about their childhood houses and she nodded as she remembered everything he recalled—the sleeping arrangements, the outhouse at the farm, the chicken coop in a room off the kitchen that later became the bathroom, the washtub that served for bathing until the bathroom was installed.

We left her with our peace, blessings, and love. We are sad but it is not because she will die to this life and journey to a new dwelling place. We are sad because we will miss her, and because we won't have another chance to tell her that she is beautiful, or to take her hand in ours to show her that we care about her, or to tell her that we love her.

Her new life will offer more glimpses of our Creator, the One who loves us forever and who cherishes us more than we can imagine. It will take another lifetime to better know the Great Dreamer who fashioned the universe and made us part of it. Many paths lead us to the Holy Breath, to feeling the Presence for a second before disappearing. It assures us that a search will continue beyond this life.

Even for those who believe in another life beyond the one we know, the passing can be fearful because it takes us to an unknown place, so breathe your peace and love to her, and breathe serenity to face her future unafraid. And show your care for members of your family with a word or touch that lets them know you love them.

Love to our Healer-Breathers,

Grandma and Grandpa

80

Nature's Magic

June 14, 06

Dear Grand Children,

Nature is spreading magic, and we are wondering whether you have noticed it, too?

Our Maple trees have tossed millions of blossoms and now are shedding the helicopter seeds, and some of them are caught on our roof where a metal lip above the porch door deflects the rain water. We sweep them up by the buckets from our patio, and the Robins, thinking our yard belongs to them, rummage through the ones on the roof looking for juicy morsels. They flick them with their beaks and the seeds float to the patio in mounds. Grandpa cheers for the Robins because then he doesn't have to clean the seeds off the roof. Meanwhile, Grandma keeps sweeping them up.

Two young, playful squirrels in our front yard like the helicopter seeds, but there is no way they and their family can eat them all. I wonder how those seeds would taste in a garden salad for humans.

Maples are sprouting—in our gardens, in the cracks in the sidewalks and between patio blocks, in all the bare spots in our lawn, and we see them growing in neighbors' roof gutters. Those seeds are programmed to live, and whether we like it or not, they are magic. That doesn't mean we have to enjoy them!

Recently we were at the Maniaci cottage where dark blue-black birds with white breasts were showing off for us. They would circle over the lake and glide toward us, showing us their backs with iridescent dark blue feathers, sparkling sequins caught by sunlight. While we toured the lake on the pontoon boat, the birds followed and circled, and when we docked, they buzzed Grandpa. Watching more closely, we discovered they built a home in a long pocket of the canvas top, and we were taking their brood for a ride on the lake as well! They must have been happy to see us leave.

Our Clematis vine is the home for a pair of Robins who built their nest where we can observe them. One evening we counted four blue eggs, and the next morning there was at least one gray downy ball. Now the nest is filled with gray down, open beaks and feet, Mama and Papa Robin constantly feeding them. Mrs. Robin scolds us when we come too close.

The world is filled with Nature's magic and mystery, even when these miracles are not especially appreciated!

OXOXOXOX,

Grandma and Grandpa

81

Robins

July 2, 06

Dear Grand Children,

Our nest of robins is vacant. We were at the Maniaci cottage last week, and when we returned home, we found the abandoned nest.

Robins will have two or three families every year. The mother builds the nest with a little bit of help from dad. Sometimes they use the same nest, but our robins must have chosen another spot. The mother sits on her nest that usually has four blue eggs. When the brood hatches in about two weeks, they are without any feathers but quickly develop the gray down that we saw. It takes only two more weeks, and sometimes less than that, for them to develop into a size where they can leave the nest. That is a lot of growing up to do in four weeks!

Dad takes over their education when they leave the nest because the mother is starting the whole process of nesting again. The juveniles follow dad around and beg for food, but dad weans them by putting some morsel of worm or insect or berry at their feet for them to pick up. They soon learn that dad does not always listen to their begging chirps. At night, the youngsters roost with their dad and other robins and at the end of the nesting season, mom joins them.

We see robins in our yard and wonder whether they came from the nest in our clematis vine. We have seen several robins swoop and dip in formation like airplanes. How can they swerve and plunge together without flying into each other? The dads sing during the nesting season, but very little during the fall and winter months. What tells them when to sing?

A few years ago, when we were growing up, we remember dark moving clouds of birds in their migratory flights. Then something happened. Birds and insects became scarce. During the 1960s Rachel Carson who was a marine biologist, wrote a book, *Silent Spring*. In it she described what was happening to nature because of the dangerous chemical, DDT, which we were using to control insects. You already know that what we do to one part of nature affects everything else in nature. We were spraying to get rid of some pesky insects, but those insects were dinner for the birds, and then we lost their songs. The U.S. eventually banned the lethal (deadly) insecticide. Birds are becoming more numerous, but not yet like the swarms we remember.

So is this the end of the story on birds? No, because a pair of Cardinals have made a nest in the bush by our bedroom window. The nest has two eggs, white with dark speckles, and it is not easy to imagine two birds in that tiny nest. We have another bird family to watch, so stay tuned for another report!

With love,

Grandma and Grandpa

82

New Wheels

July 3, 06

Dear Grand Children,

We have new wheels; not a skateboard, not a motorcycle, not a bicycle, not a wheelchair.

We said goodbye today to our faithful Grand Marquis, the car with the convertible-look top. It was easy to spot that car because of its size, color, and canvas top when we had to search for it in a parking lot. It took us on a month-long trip five years ago, and to Winnipeg, Denver, Minneapolis, Milwaukee and the Maniaci cottage many times. We will miss the smooth ride and the space.

Our new car is a Honda Civic, "desert mist" color, a beige-gray that is not very distinctive but will "not show the dirt" according to Grandpa. It should get good gas mileage, important because we won't have to fill it as often and because it will be better for the environment.

Grandma was the first to drive it; Grandpa was magnanimous (generous) in allowing her the first chance to goof up. It is easy to accelerate (go fast quickly) and difficult to hold it to the speed limit. But as we both noticed, the digital speedometer is in plain sight for everyone to see, so we can't pretend we don't know how fast we're going.

Now we should be able to zip into parking spaces and maneuver better in tight spots. We will have to pack more carefully when we go on trips because our new trunk holds much less.

With the press of a button, the radio automatically locates the stations that are available when we out of range of our choices. That could make our trips rather dull because we won't have to search for them any more. Another radio feature is that when the traffic noise is quiet, the radio softens. How much fun will that be when we don't have the radio blasting at a stop sign? We also have a CD player, and the whole radio/ CD is anti-theft; someone trying to steal it will have to know that it won't function if it is taken out of the car. The sales person told us about the anti-theft feature, but he doesn't come with the car to pass on this information to potential thieves!

The next time we come to see you, you may not know who it is because the car will not be familiar to you. Look for a sporty car in a drab color with "H" on the front and back, and it may be us!

OXOXOXOX,

Grandma and Grandpa

83

Breathe

July 14, 06

Dear Grand Children,

How many times have we breathed peace, love and healing to you? How many times have you breathed the same to us? This is an easy way for us to feel connected to you.

This way of praying has been around for a long time. Our ancestors called it meditation. It has been used by Christians, Jews, and Muslims but it does not belong to any religion.

To pray this way is easy. Most people close their eyes. Next, get comfortable without slouching, and then pay attention to your breathing. Find the right kind of breathing for you, whether it is fast or slow, deep or shallow. Breathing is nature's way of keeping us healthy. As you breathe in and out, you can become aware of the places of energy in your body, and your mind can detect places of pain. So meditation connects us to ourselves. Think about the places of energy and pain within you for a minute.

Then the first thing you say to yourself is "May I be truly peaceful." This is not selfish because this is the meaning of "having life more fully" that is mentioned in the bible. It is what the Divine wants for us and this is what you want for others. You can change the prayer for yourself for whatever it is that you need for the day. It can be for healing, understanding, happiness, safety, honesty, courage, energy, and so much more.

Take some time to think about peace. It is not found in the past or in the future. It only comes in the present, at this moment. Then think about how peace comes to you. You cannot rely on any person or any thing to bring you peace; you must rely on yourself, on what is within you.

Imagine air infiltrating Earth Garden, flitting and dancing and sometimes whistling in and through every speck of space. It is the same air dinosaurs breathed when they lumbered on Earth Garden scrounging for food. Our ancient grandparents who lived in the first towns of Mesopotamia also breathed this air. The impure air you breathe out is transformed by plants into air that keeps you alive, so plants need you and you need plants. Our breathing connects us with everything, and without everything working together we have an ailing Universe. Even though we are responsible for our own peace, it is easier to have if it surrounds us. Breathe out peace for the Universe.

Distractions will take you away from your meditation on peace, but gently bring your mind back to it. Be persistent and don't let your mind tell you that if your friend only had shared some cookies with you, you would be peaceful. Keep bringing your mind back to peace within yourself, and peace within the Universe.

Gently come out of meditation, back to the outer world.

Spend five minutes meditating. Gradually add more time until you have fifteen minutes praying this way. It is helpful to meditate when you can't fall asleep at night, when you are worried about something, or before a big test. You can meditate in bed, at school, in a chair, on the floor, in a car.

Our atmosphere is one gigantic lung, keeping us healthy, refreshing us, and connecting us to all of Creation—to all that came before and to all that will come after us.

When we are aware of our breathing, we have the power to change our thoughts and refresh our bodies. We breathe in to transform that which is toxic inside us into peace, love, forgiveness, and healing. We can send it out everywhere on our breath, and our Earth Garden will become a better place

Love to our Divine Breathers,

Grandma and Grandpa

84

Numinous Delights

Aug 6, 06

Dear Grand Children,

Numinous (NEW-min-us). We had to look up the word when we read it in a book. It means something that has the feel of being holy; something that gives us a feeling of awe, for example, by looking at an object in creation.

We live in a numinous world. Everything in nature is holy because everything comes from the Spirit of the Universe. Our yards with trees and plants and animals are numinous. Our families, friends and enemies are numinous.

"Hold on," you might say about calling our enemies numinous, and we're with you there. It might be a stretch to call them numinous. Our enemies are threatening to us because they are bigger or more willing to fight, or like to bully people, or they might just want to make us feel humiliated and not worthy of their friendship. No matter how they threaten us, though, it is also true that our enemies have the same Life-Spark that we have. But they have made choices that make us fearful of them, and we are not able to see the numinous in them. We can decide to deal with this fear by breathing them peace and love.

Yesterday, we were aware of the "numinous" in our back yard. We watched a green hummingbird flit from one flower to another sampling the nectar. In the same garden, a butterfly bigger than the hummingbird also fluttered around, and for good reason; it was a pleasant day and the flowers were a variety of color and taste. The butterfly was some sort of Swallowtail with iridescent blue spots on the lower part of the wings. We were lucky to be able to watch these two beautiful cousins enjoying our garden.

This morning on our walk we hiked through a patch of clover and other wild flowers, some yellow buttercups, some with a small pale lavender bloom, and a few that match the dandelion flower but with a different stalk that carries more than one blossom. We have such a variety of life in our world that it is impossible to see everything and even to know about everything that we see!

When we become good observers, our Earth Garden reveals the numinous in the things we see, taste, touch, smell, and hear. When we use our senses to discover the enchanting world around us, we are sensing our Cosmic Dreamer, and we might say, "Wow!" "Awesome!" "Unbelievable!"

Love to our Awesome Numinous Delights,

Grandma and Grandpa

85

More Odds and Ends

Aug 20, 06

Dear Grand Children,

Tuesday I put the first dent in our new car which is not even two months old. On my way home from the mall a car backed into my lane from a parking spot. A big van blocked the vision of both of us, and by the time I saw it and slammed on the brakes, it was too late to prevent a collision. Our right front bumper and the right back bumper of the other car were dented but ours was worse. It has been a long time since we have had an accident, so I am grateful that it was not more than that. You can't imagine how many phone calls we have had to make to the insurance company about the accident. We are waiting for an "insurance adjuster" to look at the damage on our car.

A few days ago we noticed a grasshopper on a porch screen. It seemed to be stuck there. The next day it was still there but in a different spot. Do you think it was afraid of heights? A day later, while Grandpa was watching a football game on TV, he saw a bird swoop down and pick the grasshopper right off the screen. Yesterday a bird, a sparrow or wren, visited us for a short time at the same screen, looked at us, and quickly flew away. Maybe the bird thought we should have supplied another grasshopper.

This morning I was gathering a kohlrabi and an eggplant from the garden and watched the bees and a butterfly, a tiger swallowtail, collect nectar from our plants. It would not be an exaggeration to think that there were one hundred bees swarming the anise plants in our garden. It didn't matter to the butterfly that there were so many more of them.

In fact, the butterfly glided in a circle around me as if to say "notice me." It was painted a spectacular, showy yellow with black edging and black bars melting into the yellow wings, a large butterfly that sampled more than just the anise plants. The honey those bees are making should taste delicious because the anise leaves make a sweet, licorice-like tea, but I'm not that brave to try to discover their hive.

Your California cousins are back in school. And you other grand children must be anticipating an exciting school year! We wish you all good adventures and some pleasant challenges that will connect you with our Earth Garden. We are still fascinated with the miracles that happen in our yard. Just think of everything beyond our fence that we have missed in our lifetimes!

We breathe you peace and love in your adventures,

Grandma

86

Autumn

Oct 26, 06

Dear Grand Children,

Autumn is slipping away. Gentle breezes have escorted many leaves to the ground, exposing branches and the summer's nests. The squirrels are scurrying to bury the black walnuts that have fallen from our trees, some they will dig during winter's tough weather and some that will sprout (squirrels forget, too!) and try to "spring" from the ground when the sun warms our northland during the next growing season.

One day as we were sitting outside reading while the days were unseasonably warm, we heard a chirping sound. To us, it sounded like a squirrel. We finally spied the source, a little black and white woodpecker with a red throat. It was backing down our soft maple tree pecking away at the food it found, and every time it took a hop backwards, it made the "chirp" sound. It reminded us of a dump truck that beeps when it moves in reverse! Did you ever stop to think about the capacity of the lungs of birds? They produce a sound vibrant and melodious—or vibrant and squawky— that carries for one or two blocks, and then is answered by someone in its family. We are grateful that your lung capacity is not the same as birds if the sound you made were multiplied by your size!

On another fine autumn afternoon, we heard another voice. It was a squirrel. Every time it swished its tail, it let out a chirp. Can you imagine the tail flipping and switching, brushing and curving, and every time it moved, the squirrel complained? By the end of the afternoon, it must have been hoarse. We think that one of its family was caught in the neighbor's yard. It was making a different sound, low and gravelly with a long moaning sound, and we looked for a squirrel in distress but didn't see one. Of course, it would have tried to hide from us.

We are seeing more flocks of birds, one yesterday feeding in the neighbor's yard. Then, as if they all knew what to do, they all took flight, swooping together to come next door and feed on that lawn. Our birds are recovering a bit from the knock-out they experienced with the pesticides we used to control varmints and insects in the 1950s and 1960s.

Our flower "beds" have become just that—sleeping spots for the plants that die after the first hard frost. We dream of the next growing season, anticipating and wondering which species and colors will return to delight us after winter's slumber. For perennials, it is necessary for them to die in order to experience new life; hmmm, that is true for humans, too!

We breathe peace and love to our delightful young sprouts,

Grandma and Grandpa

87

Halloween

Dear Grand Children,

Did you ever wonder how Halloween, this fun "trick or treats" day for children began? Well, this is what we know!

To the ancient Celts, October 31 was the last day of the year, and they thought that ghosts and goblins came out of hiding to frolic on that day, so the Celts left them food and drink. They also must have had fun dressing up in costumes, some representing the ghosts and goblins, and some representing animals. Pope Gregory III wanted to change that into a Christian tradition. Does that sound familiar? Remember how Christmas began as an ancient tradition long before Jesus lived? So the pope encouraged people to offer food and drink to the poor in their neighborhoods. He also encouraged them to dress as saints, a tradition that some Catholic schools still practice on this day.

Puritans came to our country before it was known as the United States. They left England because they were harassed (bothered, ridiculed, found it difficult to live the lifestyle they wanted). Religious persecution was going on in England at the time, so after their journey to the New World they tried to outlaw Halloween because they wanted to get rid of any memories of their harassment.

For the Irish Celts, coming to the U.S. in the 1840s and later, Halloween was one of the celebrations they brought with them. Barn dances and apple bobbing became ways that families enjoyed Halloween, but around 1900, it was becoming more and more a children's holiday.

This day has changed since we were children. We would knock on doors and say "Eats or we soap!" We didn't realize until much later that we should have carried a bar of soap with us—you all know what we mean by a bar of soap? Today you still can dress up and become someone else,—spooky, scary, funny, delightful, flighty, clownish, bad, beautiful, or bold! We know that even your parents have dressed up and greeted the excited little bats and robins at your door with a magical wand or Darth Vader mask! This is the day you dare to scare, and be brave tonight so that you don't run screaming from the ghouls you meet. And best of all, this is the day you get to share your candy with your parents!

OXOXOX to our Brave Widgets,

Grandma and Grandpa

88

Sarah and Mike's Wedding

Nov 7, 06

Dear Grand Children,

This week is very special to your Aunt Sarah and your soon-to-be Uncle Mike Bird. They will be married November 11 in Zihuatanejo, Mexico, so some of you will experience the beauty of the area when you come to be with them for their wedding celebration. If you are not able to come for their wedding, you can breathe them love, peace and harmony.

This is a prayer, too, that you can say for them.

PRAYER FOR SARAH AND MIKE'S WEDDING

Holy and loving Spirit of the Universe,
You are present with us always, and today
You smile as we joyfully gather to witness
The love and devotion that Sarah and Mike
are promising to each other.

Divine Creator, your lavish blessings
cannot be contained
As they are poured out on Mike and Sarah
who continue their walk together,
partners caught in your web of Creation
that spans our Universe and beyond.

Cosmic Dreamer, you delight us with the splendor
of this place,

The water that quenches, cleanses, refreshes, and
relaxes us,
our cousin plants and brother animals found
in this Eden,
The evening sky that dazzles us, this bit of heaven
that Sarah and Mike discovered and wanted to share
with us.

Divine Lover, you cherish Mike and Sarah and walk
with them.
Their adventure continues as they uncover harmony
and beauty
that surrounds them, wonder and mystery that is
within them,
the holiness of all that can be seen, heard, tasted,
smelled, felt,
And the rapture of living that encompasses all.

Love and blessings,

Grandma and Grandpa

Sarah & Mike's Wedding

Sophia Elaine Bird - April 23, 2009

Mary, Teresa, Sarah, Becky Grandma, Jen

Tree House (Casa de arbola)

89

Gordo

Nov 30, 2006

Dear Grand Children,

"Gordo." When we were in Zihuatanejo for Sarah and Mike's wedding, many Mexicans murmured this when they saw Luke. They would pat him on the head, and smiling, would quietly mutter that word.

The people in Zihuatanejo loved children, and most would surreptitiously (ser-rep-TISH-us-lee, trying not to be seen) pat children's heads while they walked past. They obviously had a trust of each other with children, because we saw parents who would walk away from them to talk with a friend and not look worried for their child. It seemed the whole city was protecting the ninos.

Other terms that were used often at Casa del Arbol (Treehouse) where some of us stayed and where Mike and Sarah's wedding reception was held, were "muchas gracias," "muy bueno," and "buenas días;" thank you very much, very good, and good morning (or good day). We spoke them often to the staff who took care of the kitchen and laundry and the cleaning up. If you ever get the opportunity to visit Mexico, you would be smart in taking Aunt Jen with you because she knew how to ask for items to buy, how much they cost, and to ask for directions. She also could understand their answers!

Many people in that city know some English words because of all the tourists from the U.S. There are 500 taxis in that city of 100,000 people, about the size of Rochester. (Rochester maybe has 50 cabs.) It is important for them to be able to communicate with the tourists.

Other Spanish words are easy to figure out. "Playa" is added to many restaurants and areas along the beach; it means "beach." "Casa" indicates house or place to live; Casa Sun and Moon was one of the hotels along the beach.

We communicated with hands, smiles, nods, and once we received a frown from a man who thought we were exceeding our limits by getting a broom and dustpan from the maid's closet. One morning as we were enjoying the early sunrise, we observed a large woodpecker, gray with a wide red collar, getting its breakfast from a desert plant next to the veranda. The caretaker walked by, and he, too, saw the woodpecker eating; pointing to the bird, he made the motions of food going down his throat.

Back to "gordo," the dictionary has a similar word in English; gorge (gorj), meaning to eat more than enough or to stuff to capacity. If you guess that gordo means fat, you are correct!

With love, abrazos y besos por nuestros nietos,

Abuela y abuelo

90

Christmas in Rochester

Dec 30, 06

Dear Grand Children,

Christmas blew in and out of our lives in a whoosh this year. We are happy that you were able to spend time with us and with all your cousins except for the three out of high school. The last time you were all together was over a year ago, and, like sprouts, you have grown taller and have changed in other ways, so it is good to become reacquainted.

One of grandma's favorite memories is at the National Eagle Center in Wabasha, where some of you viewed Eagles close-up. For the little grandchildren, those Eagles were BIG and a bit scary when they flapped their wings while they ate.

Our large feathered cousins are a sacred symbol to the Native Americans who consider the award of an Eagle feather for an act of bravery to be the highest honor. They believe that as the Eagle soars in the sky, it is close to the Great Spirit and is a messenger to God for them. An Eagle's wing-span can be eight feet, and the balance of those wings reminds Native Americans of the balance between men and women who need the strengths and abilities of each other. An Eagle feather is shown as much respect as the sacred things in our churches.

As we all know and as Native Americans keep reminding us, we and our culture depend on the environment. We depend on our brother plants and sister animals as well as our cousin birds. Can we get along without plants and animals and birds, or would they be able to get along better without us? Our Native American family thinks that if something happened to the human family, nature would survive, but the human family would not survive without nature.

Some Native Americans believe that it is time to share some sacred traditions of our cultures. Native American leaders have said,

"The four colors of man will be coming together to unite and heal. Creator has given different gifts and responsibilities to each of the four colors. Ours is to help preserve Earth for all the children."

Christmas, the time that reminds us of the promise of children,— their enchantment of the Universe as they explore it, their ability to create and renew, their energy, the new possibilities they discover,— brings us hope for our survival and a new glimpse of the Cosmic Dreamer. We are so pleased that you were with us this Christmas.

Breathe peace and love with us,

Grandma and Grandpa

91

Interesting Discoveries

Jan 5, 07

Dear Grand Children,

We have made some interesting discoveries since you left us after your Christmas visit. Our crèche (*kresh*, French word for Christmas crib set) acquired a new sheep; this one is made out of wood and it had been in our toy box. We were terrified of a HUGE white spider in our bathroom until we discovered that it really was a plastic ring and too small for our fingers. Some Aveda conditioner to relax tangles was left in one of the bathrooms, not a help to either of us. A little block with "9" and "Peacock" on its sides is a replica of the one Jackson brought with him, and an extra pillow is at home with us until someone claims it. Hmmm—are there any other surprises we should be discovering?

Other things have happened since you all left. More dust bunnies are appearing on our wood floors, probably because they can land now without being stirred up by a lot of activity! We thoroughly enjoyed your gingerbread houses, and still have some of the candy from them, which promises to put their marks on our waists and thighs while we pretend that our clothes are shrinking.

We have discovered, too, that silence can be deafening, so we bring more CDs home from the library, not entirely filling the void of your giggles and quick bursts of energy, but soothing and at times surprising. When one discovery is gone, another one is always waiting to be noticed, and all are valuable.

We also have noticed that our house got larger when you left, more than adequate for two people. While you were here, it reminded me of the "Old Woman in a Shoe who had so many children she didn't know what to do" with kids hanging out of her home and climbing on it and getting some "broth without any bread" from her. Can you imagine how our house must have looked to our neighbors while you all were here? They, too, discovered something about us and our rambunctious (lively) family.

Snow fell late in the day on New Year's Eve, drifted down and made everything sparkling and new. Most of it is gone now, but today the sky, the direction of the wind, and atmospheric conditions threaten us with another coat of magic. We can see little flakes that seem to rise and fall, and rise again as the wind swoops and sweeps them playfully. The Cosmic Dreamer is enchanting us once more this winter.

With gratitude for discoveries and love for you,

Grandma and Grandpa

92

Change and Aunt Mick

Jan 12, 07

Dear Grand Children,

Imagine what it would be like to stay the same even though you like yourself just the way you are today. You wouldn't grow or learn anything new, you wouldn't learn new basketball and hockey moves, or discover other new talents you have. Change is an adventure. You can anticipate it (look forward to it) eagerly or you can cringe (back away) from it in fear. We do both, anticipate and/ or cringe, when we face something new or different in life, because every day we have choices that lead to adventure.

My Aunt Mildred Mraz died last week in Florida. We called her Mick because it was a shortened version of her maiden name (last name before she married), Mikulecky (MICK uh lets key) and because my mother, your great-grandmother—was also named Mildred. Your great-grandmother was called Mil or Milly, but I called her mom.

Twice during my high school years I visited Aunt Mick and Uncle George with some relatives, three of us teenagers and five of us all together. It was a great treat to visit them, although they ended up sleeping on the floor to accommodate all of us. Teenagers can be challenging, but they handled us well. Hmmm, does that mean we got our way? Not always.

Aunt Mick and Uncle George owned a hardware store in Millersburg, Ohio. Many Amish lived on farms in the area, and they often visited their store, riding in horse-drawn buggies. The women wore bonnets and the married men grew beards.

During those years I remember Mick as a wary passenger whenever she rode in a car. "George!" she would say frantically whenever she thought we were on the brink of a disastrous accident. A teenage mind never envisioned the outcome the way she did. We would tease her about it, and George smoothed the situation easily.

When they retired, they moved to Tampa, Florida. Your Mayer parent will remember Aunt Mick and Uncle George because we met them in Tampa's Bush Gardens amusement park one day during our Christmas vacation. It rained while we were there and we ended up cold and wet. They invited us to their house where Mick gave us other clothes or robes and put ours in the dryer. At their table with all the chairs they owned, we were barely able to fit around it. You will have to ask your parent what we ate that evening because I have no clue!

Mick always sent a chatty Christmas note, telling us of her son Jim and daughter Joyce and their families, and the activities she and George enjoyed. They were volunteers during their retirement years and participated in Senior Citizens gatherings. George passed on to new life several years ago from a sudden heart attack, and then Mick moved to Tallahassee with her daughter Joyce. There was no note this Christmas.

Aunt Mick was fun, and she had a great laugh and smile. If she ever became angry, it was never around us. She was a caring person, one with lots of patience and always welcoming. Recently she began using a walker and caught pneumonia in December. At 89 years old, her life with us was becoming more difficult. She missed George after he died, so just imagine the wonderful reunion she must have had with him and the ancestors who went before her, all part of our Cosmic Spirit's family. Her life is changed, not ended, and she is met now with great rejoicing.

Breathe love and peace to her and her family with me,

Grandma

93

Cherokee Story

Feb 24, 07

Dear Grand Children,

How time flies when you are having fun! And so is your school year passing quickly because you're having fun? The time we were in Milwaukee last week flew while we enjoyed playing "hide" with Jackson who thinks that's what he is doing when he runs around or peeks underneath the coffee table at us. It is easy for him to be happy when he has someone paying attention to him and his needs.

As we grow older, it is more difficult for others to take time to pay attention to us and our needs because we are able to take care of many of them ourselves. And sometimes we can get cranky when we get the feeling that no one who matters to us cares about us. It is a passing feeling because there will always be someone who cares about us, but that "someone" also may be having difficulties.

There is a story about the two wolves that live within each of us and battle for attention. An old Cherokee grandfather—is there any grandfather who isn't old?—was talking to his young grandson. He spoke about one wolf who is quick to anger, who is selfish and envious, who feels s/he is a victim and who is resentful and is greedy and full of pride. This wolf is sad and feels no one loves him/her.

The other wolf in this battle is happy for the goodness that comes to others, who is kind and generous to family and friends, who tries to fill people with hope, peace, love, and kindness. This wolf searches for truth, is compassionate and understands how another person feels.

The young grandson thought about this for a bit, and said, "Grandfather (he didn't call his grandfather old), if there is a battle between these two wolves, which one wins?" The old grandfather replied, "The one you feed."

We know that it can be difficult to recognize the wolves that are battling for our attention, but once we become aware of it, it is easier to make the choices that will feed the wolf that brings happiness to us. You all have made good choices, so you know that when you make it possible for others to feel pleased about themselves, it makes you happy.

When you feed the wolf that brings happiness, you learn how to forgive but remember the lesson that brought the need for forgiving. You learn to hold onto the truth even when others disagree with you. You offer peace to your family and friends by avoiding conversations that belittle them even when they haven't learned that their remarks are hurtful to you. You are caring even when others are not. You realize that your happiness depends on whether you can make yourself and others happy, not on whether they can do that for you. No one, *no one* always makes the good choices, but when you keep practicing and choosing the wolf that brings happiness, it becomes easier each time.

With love to our Grand Children,

Grandma and Grandpa

94

Beauty without Asking

Feb 26, 07

Dear Grand Children,

This morning we woke up to a landscape that was laden with mounds of white frosting that looked good enough to eat, our street of gingerbread houses dressed in white. It seemed that a cartoonist drew our neighborhood and stretched our roofs taller and thicker, shrunk our fences by half their usual size, and dipped the evergreens into a courtly bow.

A plow took three runs at the small hill where we live; he became stuck at the top of the hill on the cul-de-sac and had to call for a rescue plow to dig him out. We played in the snow after the plow cleared our street, removing the snow from our driveway that had fallen during the night and early morning. It was the heaviest snow we had all winter. Saturday we had thunder and lightening and freezing rain which glazed two or three inches of snow that had fallen before the storm. It was hard to remove that icy glaze and the heavy snow that topped it. And guess what? It's snowing again!

Bad weather sometimes brings out the goodness in people. We have a neighbor who lives on the cul-de-sac who is at least 80 years old. He called to offer to drive us anywhere we needed to go because he has a four-wheel-drive vehicle. Two members of his family died a year ago, and we visited with him and took him some food, so we think he wanted to do a favor for us. He said he couldn't walk but he could drive.

Snowfalls can close down schools, and meetings may be cancelled, but the schools should be open tomorrow because the streets are plowed. Many of our snowstorms have happened on weekends so we haven't had any closings this year, but March usually is the snowiest month; school children in Rochester still may be surprised with a snow day. When we went to school, we walked because there were no school buses to take us, but each neighborhood had an elementary grade school within walking distance. We don't remember having a snow day when we were in school but we do remember high snow banks that we never minded climbing over to get across the streets. Snowfalls always seemed deeper when we were children.

This beautiful and delightful winter weekend reveals the humor in our universe, a thunderstorm coming in the middle of the snowstorm. This snow is part of the magic that happens in our world, even on days without a big storm to grab our attention. This amazing magical Earth makes us wonder about the marvelous Dreamer who set it all in motion.

Love to our Dreamers,

Grandma and Grandpa

95

We Had So Much Snow...

Mar 3, 07

Dear Grand Children,

Some of you had snow this week. How much did you get?

We had so much snow that schools were closed for two days because of it, even though on the first day we didn't have enough to use a snow-blower.

We had so much snow that the snow-blowers built a size larger than toasters were incompetent and unqualified for the job.

We had so much snow that the squirrels can't get to our birdfeeders to steal the birdseed.

We had so much snow that our ski and sledding hill in the back yard has drifted closed.

We had so much snow that we had to tunnel through it to get to the compost barrel.

We had so much snow that the mounds on our roof have morphed into weird sculptures and created stalactites on our eaves trough.

We had so much snow that the teenage football player next door got lost making snow angels.

We had so much snow that the snow plow got stuck on our cul-de-sac!

We had so much snow that the garbage haulers and newspapers were a day late.

We had so much snow that all the yards are clean and all the neighbors met again as they shoveled their way to the street.

We had so much snow on the telephone wires that our conversation took longer to transmit to the person on the other line.

We had so much snow that we changed the direction of our driveway and made our street narrower.

We had so much snow that the tracks of an exotic animal turns out to be the dog next door (who thinks it's his job to water our rose bush); he is built so low to the ground that he makes a burrow wherever he roams.

Love to our beautiful grand children,

Grandma and Grandpa

96

Magnificence

Dear Grand Children,

Flying back from San Diego last week we saw part of our magnificent country from the air. Mountains, clustered and queued (in a line) were heavily brushed with vanilla, the Grand Canyon with its deep and darkened chasm revealed brick-shaded patches of landscape to the east of it, Nebraska's soft gray sand-dunes, lakes of various shapes and sizes, and the rivers that meander through it all, all of it blending and unaware of the imaginary state lines. All of it was neat and tidy, a miniature panorama because we were seven miles high!

The people who live in our country are as beautifully diverse as our landscape, people with myriad skin shades, with many languages, with differences in what is important to them, and with many ways to worship the One who set our universe in motion and continues to be within all of Creation today. We all are blending as friends and neighbors and cannot see the imaginary lines that separate us into different states or nations.

We are becoming aware of this variety and diversity. It stretches our minds when we are shown new ways of seeing and observing, enlarges our hearts when we can appreciate other ways to celebrate with our neighbors, and it piques (peeks, entices us to think about something in a different way) our imaginations when we see different combinations of colors, foods, and ways of expressing joy and sorrow.

When we come to know a person or place better than before, we lose our fear of it or come to know where the danger lurks. If we know what pulls the trigger on someone's patience, or where there are slippery rocks along the coast, we can avoid disasters.

Each landscape has its own splendor, and so does each person! There is no mistake that magnificence is in both land and persons, sometimes hidden to us, but always there.

We appreciate your gifts of delight, curiosity, adventure, steadiness, reliability, thoughtfulness, patience, humor, honesty, forgiveness, words of healing, and so many other wonderful parts of yourselves that are not yet known. Of course, you should appreciate your gifts, too!

With love,

Grandma and Grandpa

97

Cajuns

Dear Grand Children,

Have you tasted Cajun food? Do you know why it is called Cajun?

When North America was called the "New World" in the 1600s and 1700s, French settlers made their homes along the northeast coast and called their area Acadia, which is now part of Canada. The English, too, settled peacefully in the same area, but the two mother countries in Europe began a war. The Acadians remained neutral, not taking a side in the war. Eventually, the English won and were given Acadia. The English asked the Acadians to leave within 18 months. When they didn't, the English torched their houses, and families were split up and put on ships and sold into slavery. A few Acadians managed to slip away and settle in areas further south along the Atlantic coast and along the Mississippi River, some eventually settling at the southern end of the river in Louisiana. They had married Native Americans and other Europeans, and those who settled in Louisiana married Africans from the Caribbean Islands off their coast. They became a mix of skin colors.

Cajun is a term that has evolved (come about) from the word "Acadian." When we pronounce "did you know," it becomes "didja know," and so "Acadian" became "Cajun." Ways of celebrating evolved for them too; when we are separated from our traditions we try to remember how it is done but we also create new ways to remember holidays.

In 1916, around the time of World War I, Cajuns were forbidden to use the French language in schools. When you don't use a language, you forget it. They still sang the traditional folk songs but forgot what

200

the words meant. They continued to celebrate Mardi gras, and created a new style of music that they used in their festivals.

Cooking, too, changed when the Acadians settled in Louisiana. They grew what they could and used what was available in their region. Rice became a staple because of abundant water in which to grow it. They learned to like alligator, turtle, rabbit, and frog legs. A meal usually had three pots of food,—one a main dish, one a rice or grain serving, and the third pot a vegetable.

They are famous for soup called "gumbo." Bell pepper, onion and celery are often cooked with meat or fish. Okra is a favorite vegetable from their African ancestry for their gumbo, and they experiment with herbs and spices. Some of their favorite flavorings are cayenne pepper, sassafras, garlic and parsley. You can research online by typing in Cajun to find out more about them and their cooking.

Cajuns had to make changes to survive. Since leaving their home in Acadia 250 years ago, they have forgotten some of their language, have altered their cooking habits and food preferences, and celebrate in new ways. They borrowed food, language, and festivals from the people they married and the places where they lived, and continue their hope-filled adventure of life. We learn from them that change happens and sometimes it is necessary, and that good can come from tragedy and trial. The spark of Life is creative, innovative, forgiving, and healing.

We breathe you peace and love,

Grandma and Grandpa

98

Stories of Events and Feelings

Mar 29, 07

Dear Grand Children,

The last letter explained to you what happened to the Acadians who were forced from their homes in Canada 250 years ago. Those Acadians who settled where the Mississippi River flows into the Caribbean Ocean are now called Cajun. They had to change their lives to fit their new 'hoods. Some of their old ways are lost because they no longer use them, and not many of their stories were written down.

After 50 years, our memories don't recall many details, and sometimes a story gets exaggerated. When a person says she ate a ton of food, that is an exaggeration; that person wants you to know that she ate way too much. When my Grandmother Agnes Mares Mraz was alive, I remember the kolaches (*COAL lot chez*, a breakfast pastry) she made. She used bread or pastry dough, formed a four inch square and put a heaping tablespoon of filling on the square of dough. The filling was poppy seed, prunes or other fruit. Then she pulled the four corners over the filling and pinched them in the middle to cover the filling. I didn't learn how to make them and haven't seen them in bakeries. So in two generations, 40 years, our family lost that way of making kolaches which melted in your mouth! Ok, the "melt in your mouth" could be an exaggeration.

Two stories in the newspaper today describe what happens when we want to express something that touches us deeply. One story is about a man whose pen pal was Jackie Robinson, the first black man who became a Major League baseball player. The man is retired now, but as he remembers how special this friendship was to him, he said, "It seemed like Jackie handed me a baton—a baton of friendship."

The other story was about children learning how to dance for a documentary film. They were using "Rite of Spring," composed by a Russian, Igor Stravinsky. Stravinsky often puts together notes that are not usually heard together, and his music has a definite rhythm/ beat. The students learned to like his music so well that one of them said it was "kind of weird, you feel like living inside the music now."

These newspaper stories tell how two people were so deeply moved that it was difficult for them to express how much their lives had changed because of it.

Stories are records of things that happened to us and the ways they affected our lives. Do you remember the first time you could read? The first time you used a stove? The first time you tied your shoestrings? The first time you said "no?" These events changed your lives. You began thinking for yourself, became more independent, and learned new skills. Saying "no" may have made trouble for you, but sometimes it is good to say "no" when it keeps you away from trouble! We each have stories to tell about our lives, about the mystery of change and the abundant blessings that touch us with such power that sometimes we make up words or exaggerations to describe them! Splendiforous! Died and went to heaven! Beauteously!

With love to our Splendiforous Grand Children,

Grandma and Grandpa

99

Bible Stories

Mar 30, 07

Dear Grand Children,

What next? We wrote about Cajuns and their lost families and friends when they were forced from their home in Acadia and how fast changes happen. Yet, with their tragedy they found goodness. We wrote about how stories preserve some of history, and how quickly we can forget what happened to us. Other stories are etched deep in our bones, hearts and minds when they express true and lasting friendships or the magic that touches our lives. These stories are difficult to put into ordinary words because the feelings they conjure (CON joor, recall from our memories) are extra-ordinary.

With Easter less than one week away, we recall bible stories of Jesus written by persons who were deeply touched by his life. Jesus was a Jewish rebel. He learned the Jewish laws, but he thought about what they said and wondered why people followed a law that didn't make sense. If a neighbor's donkey got loose on the Sabbath,—a day of total rest according to the law—why not help him round up his donkey? Jesus was not afraid to have discussions about things like this with the temple officials. These discussions sometimes got him into "hot water."

Jesus suggested ways of dealing with the Roman soldiers who occupied Jewish land. He told his Jewish friends to cooperate, and then to make it difficult for soldiers to ask for help again. Soldiers could require anyone to carry their heavy weapons for one mile, so Jesus told his friends, "carry them two miles!" If a soldier was caught forcing someone to carry his weapons more than one mile, he was punished by the centurion, the leader of the soldiers. Jesus was clever.

Someone asked Jesus, "Who is our neighbor?" So he told the story about a guy who was robbed and left dying along the side of the road. A rabbi (Jewish official) passed him up because if this guy died while he was trying to help, the rabbi would have to go through a few days of "purification," to make himself clean. The Jewish community believed that coming in contact with a dead body made them "impure." So the Jewish law required them to use the ashes of a red heifer to make themselves clean again, and the rabbi didn't want that hassle. Another respected man, one who was born into a classy tribe, also passed by the unfortunate guy, maybe for the same reason.

A Samaritan comes along the road. A Samaritan was a person who had one Jewish parent and one non-Jewish parent. Samaritans were considered half-breeds by the Jewish community and were not respected. This low-life half-breed fellow can't pass the man dying along the side of the road. He may have remembered that the Hebrew scripture tells us to love our neighbor as our self, one of the most important Jewish laws, but the story says "he was moved to pity." The Samaritan not only stops to help, he takes him to a hotel and cares for him. So in the end this half-breed low-life who may have been spit upon by someone like the dying guy, recognized him as a brother, a neighbor, and is full of mercy for him.

To Jewish listeners who came from classy tribes, this story did not fill them with a lot of love for Jesus because it bothered their egos. But to Jesus' followers, they could see the truth of the story,—do what we would like to have done to us; be caring, compassionate, merciful, forgiving, loving.

The Bible stories have very little about Jesus growing up or about his parents, whether he had a girlfriend or whether he went to school. The stories that remain are memories about a man who lived twenty to seventy years before anything ever was written down about him. So you can imagine how much was lost about his life. What remains is the power of the friendship that grew from knowing him and the mysterious, magical, mystical change that it brought to those who came to know him.

Love to our Magical Mystics!

Grandma and Grandpa

100

Happy Easter

Apr 4, 07

Dear Grand Children,

So how are you going to celebrate Easter?

For followers of Jesus, it is a time to remember. Nothing was written down for more than twenty years after Jesus died, so many memories about him are lost. What is remembered is how Jesus touched other people's lives, and how he spent time listening to the Spirit. He is remembered for speaking the truth even when others wanted to hide it. It was risky for him to be truthful because eventually he was brought to trial for things the Jewish leaders claimed he said and then sentenced to death as a criminal.

Jesus was a person like us. He called us brothers and sisters in the huge family of God. He said we could do all the things he did, only better. He said we can heal others by being caring and loving and peace-filled and forgiving. Jesus died and we will too.

Whoa, you say. Isn't there more to the life of Jesus? What about the story telling us that Jesus was raised from the dead and lives?

All of the stories of Jesus came from his Jewish friends. They searched the Hebrew Scriptures and wrote the gospels using Hebrew language taken from the psalms and prophets to help them say how they felt about Jesus. These stories developed into versions that do not agree on details.

The Easter stories tell of an empty tomb and a stone rolled away from its entrance, an angel or two, women who couldn't find his body, spices to anoint him. These details are not important. What was important to those early writers was portraying Jesus as the one who led them to a loving and caring God, to a God who is not in the sky but in the deepest part of our hearts.

Jesus is remembered for his love and generosity. He is remembered for leading his friends to the place within ourselves where the Divine Creator can be touched. He brought a new way of living, of pouring out *love that multiplies as it is spent*, a new way of becoming fully alive to the One who beckons us to shed our fears and regrets.

He taught his followers that we all belong to the family of God, the One who overwhelms us with a love that began before we were born, and that love will never go away! God, the Spirit of Life, blesses us with more gifts than we can examine and explore! Like Jesus, we are invited to live and love fully, now and beyond this lifetime. Happy Easter!

We breathe peace and love to our Blessed Grand Children,

Grandma and Grandpa

101

Easter Symbols

Apr 5, 07

Dear Grand Children,

Ham and eggs and Bunnies. Why do you think these are used to celebrate Easter?

During the time when stories were told—before people ever knew how to write them down—people worshipped many gods and goddesses. They worshipped the Sun because of its gifts of warmth and light. They worshipped the rain god and goddess because rain nurtures plants and refreshes Earth. They worshipped the love goddess and called her Queen of Heaven. They realized the influence of the moon in the world and called Earth their Mother. They saw how Nature provided the things they needed and so they had many gods to thank.

The Goddess of Spring has many names. She is called Astarte by some, Ishtar by others. Spring is the time when Earth blossoms into abundant new life, so our early ancestors celebrated this renewal. Look at the goddess names again and see if you can detect the word "Easter."

In Babylon, Tammuz was part-god and part-human who was worshipped for abundant life. He died in autumn and was reborn in the spring. Our ancestors would begin their spring festival with fasting. Carrying a figure of Tammuz in procession, they sang songs of mourning. As the sun went down, Tammuz was buried, and the singing continued. At dawn, a fire was kindled, the tomb was opened, and Tammuz was reborn. His rising from the dead was a sign of new life, and it was celebrated with joy and delight.

Some of our celebrations of Easter are borrowed from the ancient people, and their symbols recall for us the miracles of birth, death and resurrection. Eggs suggest birth and resurrection, the transformation from death to life. Rabbits are known for their large families suggesting abundance. The pig was good luck, so they served ham (smoked pig) at this celebration.

Jesus tells us in the gospel stories that we, like him, are members of the Divine Family. We are "Home" for the Cosmic Dreamer who loves us more than we can imagine. We carry on the Dream by honoring and loving others in the Global Family, and by treating them as we want to be treated. Like the ancient ones, we celebrate the promise of new life at Easter time. We welcome our own transformation as we follow the path of Jesus, and celebrate his resurrection and Nature's renewal.

Our ancient ancestors were very bright! Happy Season! Happy Easter!

With love to our own Symbols of Rebirth,

Grandma and Grandpa

102

Wickedly Chocolate

Apr 28, 07

Dear Grand Children,

    Last evening we had some friends come for supper and then they stayed for a meeting. We made the dessert that was a huge success. It was wickedly chocolate-chocolate. So I'm sending you the recipe. Like last evening, you probably should serve (and eat) soup, salad and bread before you try the wickedly delightful stuff.

> **Chocolate Pudding Cake**
> Preheat oven to 350 degrees and lightly butter a 9 inch cake pan
> Melt together –
>   2 TBS butter or oleo
>   2 oz unsweetened chocolate (or substitute 8 TBS unsweetened cocoa powder and 2 TBS butter or oleo)
> Mix together -
>   1 Cup flour
>   2 tsp baking powder
>   1 tsp salt
>   ¾ Cup sugar
> Stir the melted ingredients with the dry ingredients.
> Mix together and add to the other ingredients
>   1/2 cup milk
>   1 tsp vanilla

Optional; add - ½ to ¾ cup chocolate chips (we added them)
Press this mixture into the greased pan; it will be stiff and not easily pour out.

Topping
Stir together and sprinkle over the top of the cake
  ½ cup brown sugar
  ½ cup white sugar
  ¼ cup unsweetened cocoa powder
Pour over all - 1 ¼ cup boiling water.

Bake for about 40 minutes until the sides begin to pull slightly away from the pan; begin checking on it after 35 minutes. Serve while warm.

This might be very addicting! We don't recommend eating it more than once a week unless your parents give their consent.

Love to our Adventurous Bakers,

Grandma and Grandpa

Ben with Kelli & JD

Grandpa with Sarah & Ben

Erica

Becky & Ben

212

Aunt Agnes, Mildred & lunch pail

103

Unwelcome Guest

May 2, 07

Dear Grand Children,

Yesterday morning we had an unwelcome cousin visit us with an unfamiliar name to you, from the Chiroptera family. It was a BAT. Oy vey! (That's a Jewish expression that means "how frustrating" or "how exciting!")

Cousin Bat Chiroptera was hanging upside down between a window pane and a screen on one of our porch windows. It must have found its way inside because we don't know how it could have wedged itself there from outside. Grandma was very grateful for the window barrier because she could see the bat without it being able to fly away, or worse, towards her! We really enjoy seeing all things in nature but this cousin found its way to a place where we think it didn't belong.

It was dark brownish-gray, its little feet at the top and the wings wrapped around it so that it looked like a plump square package with tiny ears poking out at the bottom. It was about as long as our pointer finger and as wide as the thumb knuckle. We can't imagine that it found any food; some bats like fruit, but their favorite meal is overdosing on insects. They will devour 300 mosquitoes in an hour, so they are very helpful, but they have to be outside to do that!

Bats are valuable to us not only because they eat many insects but because, like bees, they also pollinate our plants. This furry cousin of ours is useful in other ways and is remarkable and valuable to us so we should be pleased that they are in our world, but NOT in our homes.

There are 1000 varieties of bats, some as small as a bumble bee, and some with a wingspan of six feet which is about as far as your Dad can reach out with his arms. That would be a humungous size and a little frightening, sort of like a dinosaur coming to say hello to you. Oy vey!

Bats usually are active at night, and use their hearing to navigate in the dark but they can see. They are wild, so we should not touch them. I don't know what happened to the one who claimed the spot on our screen, but Grandpa says he never touched the bat although it is in the backyard in a newspaper.

With love to our Inquisitive and Brave Grand Children,

Grandma and Grandpa

104

Colorado Trip

June 12, 07

Dear Grand Children,

We're back from Colorado with a little tan and a lot of happy memories. Soon after we landed at Denver airport, we set out for Steamboat Springs with the Greseth family, a three-hour drive into the mountains. We stayed in an attractive condo for a weekend adventure.

Saturday morning Jen, Lee, Morgan, Luke and we grandparents took a nature hike to a surging, white-foaming waterfall. It was thrilling for Luke as he stamped and tried to jump his enthusiasm. Mom Jen and grandma hovered over him knowing his wobbly hops could land him into the surging water. Morgan realized its strength and respected it, staying close to safety. The sun turned its spray into showers of sparkling gems. Boiling and bubbling, it absorbed all other sounds so that we had to shout to be heard. The rocks in the water's path kept the rush of water churning as it tumbled down the mountain. It was power, raw and beautiful.

In a more serene part of the walk we spied large dark-feathered birds with light breasts and heard their melodies, new for our ears. Park displays helped us identify flowers, trees and bushes. Some were familiar but others were new to us; some perfuming us, displaying their charm and asking us to notice them.

Jen and Lee had signed up for a marathon that was held on Sunday and they both won,—everyone who runs that far and finishes is a winner—finishing the 26.2 mile (40 kilometers) race in spite of being tired and weary and sore. Then they took turns driving back to Denver, and chatted and laughed all the way. It is a huge accomplishment to finish and they earned the natural "high" that comes from an event like that!

It rained the day after we returned to Denver, so Morgan and Luke took umbrellas outside to feel the downpour. By Luke's expression, he didn't appreciate the water heaving over the umbrella but Morgan boogied. What a difference from the waterfall experience!

We were treated to delicious meals by cooks Jen and Sarah while we were in Denver. Thursday the Grand Children were left at home to make cookies with their neighbor while we adults attended an outdoor concert at Red Rocks and heard Harry Connick jr. and his big band. The temperature was expected to be in the 30s so we bundled in winter wear to enjoy their New Orleans jazz improvisations.

Our tickets to return home via Midwest Express Airlines routed us through Milwaukee with a 40-minute dash to the plane for Minneapolis-St .Paul, the most economical when we bought them. At the airport we thankfully discovered that our tickets were changed so that we flew directly to MSP on United. But, as we were herded through the routine, we both were singled out for the extra check,— patted down and the inspection of take-on luggage. Grandpa had a glue stick that was confiscated. Go figure!

A nice surprise waited for us at home; our grass was freshly cut and edged by unknown elves, but an email from Uncle Andy cleared up the mystery. Aunt Ann had been here with Patty, Caroline and Tim.

We are very fortunate to have a caring family, competent with culinary knives and yard tools, and equipped with generous hearts.

Our love and gratitude,

Grandma and Grandpa

105

Mother Nature

June 12, 07

Dear Grand Children,

Someone is knocking on your door. A woman is standing there and she tells you she is Mother Nature. Hmmmm, she looks very good for being millions of years old! She has a smile on her face, doesn't need a cane, and her eyes twinkle. You invite her in, make Chai tea and offer her some oatmeal cookies.

In her conversation with you she says, "You and I have been together since the beginning of time. You are born from me, you have tasted and seen me and you know that I am good."

Yes, you understand that all things that can be seen and felt come from earth. You eat the cookie and know that everything that was used to make it originally came from Earth, from being one thing and changing to another. The cookie becomes you and eventually will decompose and return as something else.

Mother Nature continues, "I come to remind your senses, all of them, that if you stay awake to me, you will feel my gentleness and smell my fragrance. You will see my magnificence and taste my sweetness. You will hear my love-songs and you will glimpse the face of the Divine Creator.

"You and I, we breathe the same air and circulate it around the world. We are so connected we can't live without each other! When you struggle with a problem, so do I. When your soul is humming, so is mine. When you offer consolation, I do too. When your mind is nudged by my beauty and charm, I am enchanted by yours.

"You are a jewel among jewels, precious in my sight. You are my delight and I display my wonders and miracles for you, enticing you to explore and learn, to admire and create.

"Come to me when you are weary, when your burdens become too great. My home is everywhere and I give you rest and peace.

"Remember me, because when you don't, you become lost. We need each other. We absorb each other's pains and become the healing for the world. We are the oceans for love and forgiveness, reconciliation and love. We are the path for the discovery and the 'rapture of living.'

"When you are with me, you will see that your face and the Cosmic Dreamer's are the same."

We love our Divine Grand Children,

Grandma and Grandpa

Afterward

Joe and Molly were married Sept 28, 2007, with most family members being able to attend. This is our prayer for them.

Wedding Prayer for Joe and Molly

Holy Spirit of the Universe, we gather around Joe and Molly today, knowing that you have cherished and blessed them from the beginning of time. This day was woven into possibility for them as they chose your gifts and developed their curious and intelligent spirits, their delight and exuberance for life. Along the rough places on their journeys, they unwrapped tenacity and endurance as they explored your gifts of forgiveness, healing and renewal.

Loving Creator, we rejoice with you as Molly and Joe promise to continue their path of friendship, encouragement and love for each other as helpmates in marriage. Their new adventure answers the stirrings for a loving home and unites the children already in their care with their own gifts of enchantment and challenge.

We remember today your Holy Mystery, your fire of life, the spark that sustains and empowers us. Especially today we remember that Joe and Molly, carriers of your divine spark, become your peace and compassion for the world.

They are your hearts that offer humor and delight.

They are your hands that tend and support life when it needs a more nourishing atmosphere.

They become the harmony of a new song to celebrate your Creation in all its forms, the four-leggeds and cousin plants, all that is seen and unseen.

They dance in gratitude for your abundant blessings.

As Joe and Molly embark on this new path of their journey, they are not alone; they have invited us to walk with them, and here we are; we have answered "yes."

With you, Cosmic Dreamer, we lift them up to soar on your boundless breath of love.

Amen.

SINCE THESE LETTERS WERE WRITTEN, Erica Powell has become a cherished member of our family through Ben. Their concern and encouragement for each other is not only supportive for themselves but for us as well. We are pleased with their relationship and welcome her to our family.

On April 23, 2009, Sophia Elaine was born to Sarah and Mike Bird. Sarah writes: ... "I can't believe everyone trusts us to take care of this baby!!! Haven't had to call the pediatrician since day 1."

Sophia
A Conversation with Creator

Cosmic Dreamer, we are amazed at the new miracle in our midst,
given the name Sophia Elaine to claim the gifts of wisdom and light.
Your oceans of blessings for her can't be numbered,
hers for exploring a world of adventure, love, and harmony.

Born into two nurturing and supporting families,
She knits a stronger union between them
and adds her charms to the fabric begun by her cousins.
She brings us hope for the future.

She is finding her power,
softening our hearts as we recognize Your Breath through her,
and enlarging our capacity to make room
for the world that she has just turned upside-down.

Her smile heals the most needy souls;
her graceful movements a reflection of Your walk among us.
We are captured by this Enchanting Mystery who relies on us,
and welcome Sophie into our family and world.